The Shadow's Edge

The Chanters Novellas: Book 2

Rachel Song

Songbird Publishing

Book Cover by Rachel Song

To those who feel monstrous,

may you learn to embrace your shadows.

CONTENTS

Chapter 1

The dungeon reeked of silence and death.

In the depths beneath the palace grounds was a windowless block of cells, kept purposefully away from the rest of the prison. The old stone walls had been reinforced over the years, and even in the darkness, the magic wards glimmered faintly for any who cared to notice them.

Isabel Algerin cared to notice them.

She kept her distance on the narrow, darkened staircase as two guards in the red and green of Medira unlocked the door, far enough back so that they couldn't see her. Even so, the stench of foul air and human odor from the warded cell block washed over her.

Her body coiled with tension as she waited for the first guard to move through the doorway, and then the second, before slinking down the final steps behind them.

The edge of her tunic brushed against the guard's arm as he turned to haul the door shut, and for a moment, he hesitated, his eyes struggling to focus in the darkness.

She flattened herself against the wall, willing herself to fade away. The guard frowned.

"Everything all right, Estes?" the other guard called from farther up the row of cells.

"Yeah." Estes shook his head. "I thought I saw something is all. This place can really get to you after a while." He squinted again, his frown deepening, but turned to follow his colleague.

Isabel exhaled and waited until the guards with their dim lanterns of enchanted orb fire reached the end of the cells before peeling herself off the wall. That had been far too close.

She could become a part of the darkness as easily as breathing, slipping through shadows where no one could find her. It was a magic she hadn't known others couldn't do until the women of the village back home in Rendra had begun to whisper loudly about shadows and the reprobate souls who made deals with them, telling their children to run whenever Isabel came out to play. Isabel roughly pushed the memory away.

The prisoners were at the bars of their cells now, scrabbling for the bowls of slop and tankards of water the guards shoved through a slot at the bottom of the bars. Isabel already knew that there were twelve men in these cells, most of them young, most of them able to wield magic, and all from the Inetian empire north across the sea.

She knew what had happened in the Malathi pass in the southeast of Medira a few weeks before. Mediran soldiers had raided the enclave of Sorothi chanters where these men had been hiding. Half a dozen of them had been killed. But for the members of the enclave, it had been either capture or death. They had betrayed the emperor of Ineti and were planning to use the chanters' forbidden magic to assassinate the emperor and put one of his sons on the throne.

It had been a stupid plan, one that had predictably ended in disaster when the novice Inetians had let their magic erupt out of control, tearing a rift in the fabric of the world. If left unchecked, a rift of that magnitude had the potential to crack apart, creating a gateway into the realm of shadow and allowing unspeakable horrors to cross into their world.

And now, in the cells across from her, were the Inetians—criminals and traitors to their king.

One prisoner's slop half-spilled onto the dirty floor. He gave a strangled cry, his fingers scrabbling uselessly for it before it soaked into the stone. Anger surged in her gut.

No living thing, let alone a *human being*, should be kept in a place such as this.

Isabel kept to the wall, her lips pressed together in disgust, as the guards rounded the corner and handed out meals to the cells on the other side. One of them had left his lantern on a low table at the end of the row, and it cast a sickly orange glow around the space, sending grotesque shadows lurching up the walls.

Her fingers moved unconsciously to the dagger at her belt—it was a short, sharp blade with a black leather handle etched with a golden bird. It had been a gift from Cassandra, Isabel's boss and the head of the queen's intelligence network, before Isabel had left Rendra with instructions to keep an eye on the captured Inetians. The Mediran king was not known to be lenient to his prisoners, even ones who had information that pertained to Medira's security.

"This dagger was given to me in a time of need," Cassandra had said as she'd pressed it into Isabel's hand. "I hope it helps you when you need it most."

Isabel had felt the wards woven through the knife before she'd reached for it, and she'd realized with a start that Cassandra, with all her ability as the queen's shadow, hadn't known about them. The wards had spread over her fingers and wrapped up her arm, a comforting presence, whispering of protection and strength, just as they did now.

Her gaze flicked down the row of cells. They were small, hardly long enough for a full-grown man to lie down in—not that there was any bedding of any sort. Her jaw clenched. The sounds of men eating had slowed, and many of them had slumped back down to the cold, damp floor. But the man in the cell nearest her was standing just behind the bars, his arms slack at his sides. And he was staring directly at her.

Isabel's heart gave a sudden thump. He couldn't see her. She knew that—even if it looked like he was staring at her.

He was young, maybe only a little older than her twenty-one years, with golden brown skin and broad shoulders. His black hair curled around his ears and down his neck, and she could tell that he'd once been muscular but that he'd lost some of that tone in his weeks down here. His tunic was dirty and torn at one shoulder, and an unkempt black beard crept along his jaw.

He took a step closer to the iron bars, and his eyes narrowed.

He couldn't see her. He couldn't. Not down here, in the dark, where her magic worked best.

"Who are you?" the man said, his voice carrying the lilt of an Inetian accent.

In a flash, she darted across the darkness to the wall beside his cell, her knife in her hand. The protective wards surged over her fingers and twined up her arm. She poised, ready to incapacitate him if he raised an alarm to the guards.

"How can you see me?" she hissed.

The man snorted. "Should I not be able to?"

"Who are you talking to, Karim?" The man in the cell beside him was at the bars now, peering curiously into the darkness. Relief washed through her as his gaze passed right over her. He couldn't see her.

Her attention snapped back to the man in the cell. He was watching her carefully, his eyes flickering with interest. "To a shadow, apparently," he said without breaking her gaze.

Isabel matched him stare-for-stare, daring him to expose her to the guards. Her magic didn't work when someone knew she was there. If he pointed her out, she would be done for.

"This damn place," the other man muttered.

The man in the cell—Karim—waited until the other man slumped to the floor before he spoke. "So, who are you then? And what in the name of the emperor are you doing here?"

"I might ask the same of you," Isabel hissed.

His brows rose. "You want to know why *I'm* here?"

Her chest tightened in annoyance. "That's not what I meant."

"Then what did you mean?"

"I didn't mean anything," she said, hating how petty her words sounded. "Of course, I know why you're here."

He let out a sardonic laugh. "I suppose everyone in this damned place does."

She glared at him. He was a traitor to his country, one who dabbled in dark magic. She would not feel sorry for him. "You're not supposed to be able to see me," she said again.

"I gathered as much." He leaned toward her from behind the bars, one hand coming up to grip the rough metal. "We don't seem to be getting very far here."

She could hear the guards coming back around the corner now, the glow from the enchanted orb fire bobbing along the ceiling as they approached. They'd finished delivering the last of the meals. She stepped away from the cell, willing herself to disappear again.

Karim kept his eyes on her, barely squinting in the darkness, as if he could see her clearly despite the dimness—despite her magic. She raised her dagger and did her best to glare at him, to instill the idea that if he said anything, his life was forfeit.

His eyes snapped to the dagger in her hand. A surge of magic rose from the wards in the knife, and she almost gasped at the suddenness of it.

Karim started, his eyes widening. "Where did you get that?"

"What?" she said before she could stop herself. The guards were getting closer. She had to move, to follow them, to slip out behind them before she got stuck in here.

"That dagger," he said.

Her fingers tightened on the knife. She didn't like his interest in it. "What about it?"

"It's mine," he said. "I made it."

"You *made* it?" She couldn't believe what she was hearing. That claim was . . . ludicrous. There was no conceivable way he could be talking about the same knife.

He opened his mouth. Something prickled along Isabel's neck, and then the world turned to a searing flash of white. For a moment, all was still. Then the world came crashing back in with a powerful roar, like a colossal crack of thunder after lightning.

Isabel was thrown back against the wall, and she gasped, her head cracking painfully against stone. The knife would have skittered from her hand if it weren't for the surge of power from the wards twining around her arm and clamping her fingers around it.

She blinked desperately to clear the afterimage the flash had burned into her eyes, briefly pressing her fingers to her ears to still the ringing. As she focused on the darkness, she saw the guards sprawled limply on the floor by the door, the lanterns of enchanted orb fire shattered on the ground and flickering grotesquely against the stone.

There was a hiss, and the acrid scent of sulfur wafted faintly through the air.

"Get out of here!" Karim hissed from behind the cell door. There was an urgency to his tone that hadn't been there before. "You don't want to be here for this."

Air heaved suddenly into Isabel's chest. He was right. Whatever was happening, whatever magic was being worked, she did *not* want to be there for it. "What about you?" she asked.

"What about *me*?" he said incredulously. "There *is* no 'what about me'. I'll be right here when this is all over. He's here for us. But I'm not going with him. And I'd suggest you get out while you still can."

Isabel's eyes flicked to the guards lying prone on the ground. She could see the ring of prison keys on the closer one's belt. There was another flash from the other side of the cells, and a few of the men cheered raucously. Her heart gave a thud.

"Hey!" Karim called as she pushed away from his cell. His voice sounded suddenly young, like a little boy scared of the dark. She paused, though she knew she really, really shouldn't. "If I'm still here when this is over, tell the woman who gave you that dagger to get me out. She owes me."

Cassandra. "We'll see," she said, casting him a final look. His eyes were wide in the darkness, and she couldn't help but feel a tug of sympathy.

Another flash, this one just as the end of the row of cells, spurred her into motion. She leaped to where the guards had fallen, her steps sounding overly loud even in the rumbling darkness. The men in the cells were shouting now, and a white light cast strange shadows across the stone. Across the walls, the wards were shimmering and sparking in an eclectic, angry red. Fear split her gut. What in the name of the Archer was happening? No one had *ever* broken through the old wards. Power like this wasn't supposed to exist anymore.

She almost tripped to a stop beside the guards. Estes' eyes were open, his gaze unseeing. Just minutes ago, he had been a living, breathing person with a whole life before him. Her stomach churned. What kind of power could do something like this?

A shout sounded behind her, and she scrabbled for the key ring at the guard's belt and yanked it off with a clink.

The door loomed before her, heavy and wooden, riddled with wards that she doubted the guards had known were there. These were cracking and red too, spreading like wildfire. She rifled through the keys, her fingers shaking, as she tried them one at a time.

The first one rattled in the lock but didn't turn. She grunted in frustration and tried the second. This one didn't even fit. She shoved the third key in.

"Let's go! Let's get out of here!" a prisoner shouted.

She fumbled with the next key, until finally, it turned in the lock. With a desperate cry, she heaved the door open.

She clattered up the steps, hardly daring to look behind her. Whatever was going on back in the cell block was worse than the guards she might come across ahead.

She rounded a corner and darted into an alcove stacked with unused bows just as a group of soldiers clattered down the stairs, short swords drawn, their sticks of orb fire held high. She didn't think swords would be of any use down there.

When they'd passed, she started back upward. Her chest was heaving, and Isabel did her best to slow her steps as she climbed, willing herself to blend into the shadows when she could, and passing with her chin raised confidently when she couldn't. No one stopped her, not with the alarm of an escape sounding down below.

With a final desperate push, she thrust out of the putrefying darkness and into the cold air of a cobblestone courtyard. She blinked rapidly as her eyes adjusted to the sudden brightness. The back of the Mediran palace rose serenely above her with its elegant white-stone towers and marvelous stained-glass windows that glinted in reds, golds, and greens in the midafternoon sun.

A cool wind whipped against her face as she leaned against a fence at the side of the courtyard. She couldn't get the way Karim had looked at her out of her head, his face suddenly boyish and scared—couldn't stop thinking about his plea for help.

She closed her eyes, feeling the soft bite of the wind on her cheeks.

Karim's words echoed through her mind again: "I'll be right here when all this is over."

He hadn't seemed to think he would escape like the others. And more insanely, he'd said he would *stay*. But why?

As more soldiers rushed for the prison, Isabel forced herself upright, pushing down the fear that still pounded through her. None of that mattered right now. She had to get away from the prison and disappear into the palace, into her fabricated life as a scribe for the Rendran ambassador to Medira. She had to find Lady Salandris, the ambassador, and warn her about what had just happened.

Because when news of the escape did reach the king, it wasn't going to be pretty.

Chapter 2

Isabel had been right. The king was in an apoplectic fit of rage when she slid into the throne room behind Lady Salandris hardly twenty minutes later. The Rendran ambassador had made an impressive stink to the guards when they'd first barred her way, but they'd eventually let her through, albeit reluctantly.

"How could you have let this happen?" the king railed at Idris, the captain of his guard, spittle flying from his mouth. He slumped on an ornate bronze-and-gold dais at the end of the grand hall. His red tunic pinched over his swelling gut, and his round, bearded face was already purple and turning more so by the minute.

Idris hardly flinched beneath stoic brows, likely used to tirades such as this one. He opened his mouth to say something, but Lady Salandris sailed forward, her blue skirts embroidered with tiny silver flowers trailing regally behind her, her court slippers clipping purposefully down the length of the polished-wood floor.

Her dark auburn hair was swept on top of her head in an elegant knot, and her chin was tipped in an air of determination and confidence. Isabel trailed in her wake, her gray eyes roving around the hall, keeping a vigilant watch for anything that might pose a threat to the ambassador.

"Your Highness," Lady Salandris said brightly, an overly pleasant smile pasted to her face. She wasn't much younger than the king, who was approaching sixty, but the years had been far kinder to her appearance. "It is an absolute delight to see you, as always."

"Lady Salandris," the king said flatly.

An alliance had been forged between Rendra and Medira hardly a month before. The king had been little help, demanding terms he knew Rendra would never accept. But he had finally, reluctantly signed, mostly at the expert cajoling of his nephew Arphaxad Ilin Serra, who was now married to Cassandra—their marriage had been a key piece of the alliance.

"I heard commotion outside the palace," Lady Salandris said, dropping into a deep curtsy. "I thought Your Highness could give perspective on what was going on. You always go so out of your way to calm the fears of your loyal subjects."

Isabel watched the Rendran ambassador with open admiration. There was the reason she wasn't a diplomat. She could hide in shadows, sure, but she would bite off her tongue before she would give that man so much as a half-hearted compliment.

The king grunted, but he no longer seemed on the verge of complete breakdown. "It's nothing to concern yourself about, Lady Salandris," he said. "There was a problem in the prison, but it's being handled." He glared at Idris, who kept his face admirably blank.

Lady Salandris gave the king a tight smile. The woman had a will of iron.

The door to the throne room opened again, and a baby-faced soldier hurried down the length of the hall. He kept his eyes on the floor, hunching his shoulders as if that might make him less visible. When he reached Idris, he said something in a low, hurried voice that Isabel couldn't quite catch. The captain's eyes widened, and he turned to the king.

"Your Highness," Idris said. "I have just had word that there is one man still in the prison who didn't escape."

Isabel's heart gave a sudden thump.

"Then where is he?" the king barked. "Bring him here, and let's sort this cursed mess out." He glanced uncertainly at Lady Salandris, as if he had forgotten she was there. She gave him another taut smile.

"Of course, Your Highness," Idris said. "The guards have already apprehended him. He's right outside the door."

Isabel's gaze snapped to the other end of the throne room.

"Send him in," the king said.

Isabel's pulse sped up as the captain motioned for the doors to open. She knew who she was going to see before they even brought him in.

If I'm still here when this is over, tell the woman who gave you that dagger to get me out.

As two soldiers pushed him through the door, Isabel could see that his arms were bound tightly behind him. One of his cheeks was dark and purple, a mark that hadn't been before, and there was an angry red gash above his left eye. Blood trickled in a dark line from the corner of his mouth. Anger surged through her as he stumbled down the length of the hall, the guards yanking him roughly by his arms. He was in far worse condition than when she'd seen him in the dungeon not thirty minutes before.

The guards shoved him to his knees in front of the king. His chest heaved as he lifted his head to stare defiantly upward, his black eyes flashing.

"What's this one's name?" the king demanded, peering disgustedly down at the prisoner before him.

"Karim Saad of Clan Marek, Your Highness," Idris said. "The nephew of Darid Saad, who was part of Sethos Amanakar's group."

Karim jerked against his bonds at the captain's words, his nostrils flaring. Sethos Amanakar was the bastard son of the Inetian emperor who had been behind the plot to learn the Sorothi chanters' magic and depose his father.

"What did you do, boy?" the king said.

"I didn't do anything," Karim rasped. He coughed, the spasms rocking his body violently.

"Then explain to me where in the name of the archer the rest of your friends went!"

A muscle jerked in Karim's jaw. "I have no idea where they went. As you can see, I'm still here."

"You have no idea, or you refuse to tell us?" The king's voice was like ice.

"Does it make a difference?" Karim met the older man's gaze defiantly.

"Watch your tone, boy," the guard beside him spat, giving him a quick kick in the ribs. Karim doubled over, coughing again.

"Your Highness," Lady Salandris protested, taking a firm step toward the prisoner.

The king raised a hand to silence her, then waited until the coughing had subsided. "How did you break through the prison wards?"

Karim's mouth twisted. "Once again, *I* did nothing. You know as well as I do that it was the work of one of the chanters who escaped your bloody raid."

Isabel could see the king's annoyance growing again. "So, they left you behind," he said.

"I *chose* to stay behind," Karim snapped. "I want nothing more to do with the Sorothi chanters and their magic. I don't know anything."

Isabel blinked. There it was again. He'd chosen to stay behind. But why? Surely escaping the Mediran prison and certain death was better than languishing behind based on . . . on what exactly? What had happened at the enclave to turn him so vehemently against the chanters?

"They have you all fooled into thinking they're harmless," Karim continued, his voice rising. "That they just want to be left alone."

A shiver moved through Isabel at his words. She knew there were men, women, and children in the enclave whose lives had been destroyed. Not everyone had agreed with the deal that had been struck with the Inetians. And from what she understood, the chanters responsible for the deal had slipped away into the night, leaving the innocent to pay the price.

"Then what do they want?" the king asked.

Karim's eyes flashed with determination. "I can tell you everything you need to know if you grant me immunity," he said.

A seed of respect nestled in Isabel's chest.

"Just who do you take me for, boy?" The king let out a raucous snort. "I don't need you telling me what I will or won't grant you."

"It seems I'm your only source of information." Karim kept his shoulders square beneath the king's gaze. "Grant me immunity, and I'll tell you everything you want to know to apprehend the chanter behind this."

The king surged suddenly to his feet. "I will *not* be blackmailed!" he roared.

"So, you'll just let me die then," Karim said. "And you'll have lost your only chance to find the men who escaped. How do you think Ineti and the emperor are going to feel about that?"

The king's face turned white for a moment, and Isabel could see the fear plain in his eyes. He had lost the most wanted, most dangerous men in the kingdom. More than just Ineti would be furious about that.

"Get him out of here, now!" the king roared to Idris, his face turning that unorthodox shade of purple again. "Give him a good whipping and bring him back to me when he's ready to talk! Twenty lashes at least!"

"Your Royal Highness, I don't—" Lady Salandris started, but the rest of her words were drowned by Karim's wild shout as he hurled himself at the soldier beside him.

The guards in the room yelled and leaped toward the unarmed Inetian, and Idris lunged in front of the king, guiding His Highness away from the mad scramble in front of the dais. Isabel surged toward Lady Salandris, pulling on her sleeve to try and keep the woman out of the fray.

"Take him out and beat him within an inch of his life!" the king shrieked as the guards pinned Karim to the floor. "I want him begging for mercy!"

"Your Highness," Lady Salandris said, shaking Isabel off. "I must protest. He is the only lead we have on what happened to the others. A whipping of that sort might kill him. We need him for information, for leverage."

The king ignored her. "Get him out of here! I want him made an example of until he's ready to talk!"

Karim was yanked back to his feet, where he hung awkwardly between the guards. Blood trickled from his mouth, dripping onto his torn tunic. He coughed, and Isabel's heart clenched as blood splattered the floor. He raised his head, and his eyes widened with recognition when he saw her.

"Your Highness," Lady Salandris protested again. "This is a matter that is of great concern to Rendra. We need him in one piece." When the king ignored her again, she turned toward Isabel, fire in her eyes. "Get him out of here," she said calmly. "In any way you can."

Isabel gave her a nod, then faded back against the wall, allowing herself to drift among the shadows as she followed the guards who were dragging Karim out of the room. Fury coursed through her. They couldn't do this. He might be a traitor, but he had crucial information about the chanters, the enclave, the Inetians—information they couldn't afford to lose. And she still couldn't get the look he'd cast her in the dungeon out of her head. And the look of stubbornness and desperation when he'd seen her in the throne room.

A strange thrumming vibrated from the knife at Isabel's belt, and she wrapped her fingers around it, power and safety and strength flowing through her body.

She slipped along the black marble of the palace halls, the heavy gold and bronze twining up the columns a far cry from the lighter, airy feel of the Rendran palace. She kept close to the guards who flanked Karim.

She followed them around the corner and out into the courtyard behind the palace. The prison was quickly coming into view. She had to do something soon, or else they would disappear with Karim back down into the blackness.

"Hey, boy," one of the guards said, giving Karim a quick jab in the ribs. "We were given full permission to have a little fun with you."

Karim lifted his head, his eyes flashing. "I bet a coward like you would like that, beating a defenseless man."

The guard lunged toward Karim again, but one of the others shoved him back. "Don't be such an ass, Rodrigo."

"You heard the king," Rodrigo snarled. "If you don't like it, you can get out. But I'm going to have my fun." He aimed another well-placed kick at Karim's ribs.

Isabel sprang forward, her knife in her hands, its wards whispering a soothing song to her muscles and joints as she gave a quick kick to the back of Rodrigo's knees. He collapsed with a yelp of surprise. She allowed the full power of the knife's wards to flow over her, drawing as much shadow around herself as she could.

She whirled, her body vibrating with energy and power, and jabbed another soldier in the throat with the hilt of her knife. He doubled over, coughing violently. She made quick work of the other four, and for a brief moment, she was left staring down at Karim, blood pounding madly through her veins.

He gaped at her, and then a grin eased across his blood-slick face. "So, you did come," he said. "I'm touched."

"You shouldn't be," Isabel bit out. "I'm certainly not doing this for you."

Rodrigo lunged to his feet, his face a mask of rage, and before she could think, Isabel reached down to grab Karim's arm. She was halfway through snapping "get up" when the world exploded.

Something sparked where her fingers clutched his arm, and then darkness and shadow and night raged through her limbs like a wildfire, flying out into the cold air of the courtyard and turning the world into a haze of black. It was a darkness that was thick and cloying, dripping with magic and power that mingled with the distorted energy of the crackling wards in the dungeon below.

Isabel didn't have time to think, to understand what was happening. She just pulled Karim to his feet and dragged him out and away from the courtyard, from the palace, from the soldiers who were shouting and scrambling madly after them. She didn't need to see or feel or hear. Movement in this space of shadow was simple, effortless, as easy as breathing, and Isabel found that she was moving ten steps for every one. She wasn't sure if they were walking or running or flying; all she knew was that they were moving, that they needed to get away, to get to safety, far from the crackling madness behind the Mediran palace.

It was the wind that brought her back to reality, the cold whipping sharply against her skin. Her body still thrummed with magic and power and darkness, and she didn't know how to stop, how to make it go away.

Then someone was shouting beside her, and a hand, strong and sure, was wrapping around her own. Then the darkness and shadow rushed out of her like a breaking dam, roaring and crackling from her fingertips and out into the cold air, where it swirled and eddied, then dissipated into nothing.

For a moment, all was silence and absence of shadow, and she found herself staring at Karim's bloodied face in the middle of a swath of arching pines.

She swayed for a moment, her vision blurring, and with a cry of frustration at her dissipating consciousness, she collapsed to the ground.

CHAPTER 3

Isabel came to in the haze of twilight. A cold wind drifted across her cheeks as her eyes cracked open. Bare gray branches stretched like clawed fingers above her, outlined by a blank gray sky. A few remaining leaves still clung in places, and she watched for a moment as a gust of wind snagged one, sending it tumbling through the air.

Her fingers were cold, she realized with a jolt. She sat up, her hand reaching automatically for the dagger at her belt. Her pulse slowed when she realized it was still there, the wards sending a reassuring warmth through her fingers. A thick, blue-checkered quilt fell away from her body.

Something moved to her right, and then, she was on her feet, the knife in her hands. A man grunted as she shoved him to the ground and angled the knife at his throat. The wards gave off a fierce warning pulse, and she stilled, staring into Karim's startled face.

"*You*," she blurted. Her tongue was thick in her mouth, and her head pounded. It was like she had been smashed against a wall and then tossed into a sack that had been thrown off the top of a mountain.

"Yes, *me*," he snapped. He'd cleaned the blood from his face and body, and the bruises on his cheek had already turned into a mass of black, blue, and purple.

"You're still here," she said almost dumbly. The checkered blanket. Had he gotten that for her somehow? Her brows creased. How long had she been out?

"I didn't think it was wise to leave the woman who'd rescued me crumpled unconscious in the woods." His eyes flicked to the knife. "But maybe I should have."

Isabel glared at him. "I don't trust *traitors*."

His nostrils flared again. "Did you not hear a single word I said in the throne room?"

"It was still a choice you made, no matter how much you regret it now."

He heaved a sigh of frustration. "You've made your position very clear. Can you let me up now? I have no intention of hurting you. And if I've understood who you're connected to, then I doubt you want to hurt me either."

Annoyance flared in Isabel's chest. She shoved him down with her elbow as she pulled the knife back and retreated a few steps. He dusted himself off as he rose to his feet. He was wearing a sturdy green coat now over his threadbare tunic, its ends falling to his knees. He'd replaced his worn shoes with thick, fur-lined boots.

"Where did you get those?" she said, jerking her chin at his clothes.

Karim gave her a look, then reached for a nondescript pack that was leaning against a tree a few feet away. Isabel had never seen it before either. Like the blanket. Like his coat and boots.

"You know what," she said. "I don't need to know."

"Here." He pulled a thick slice of bread from the pack and handed it to her. "Eat this."

She eyed him warily. She still had no reason to trust him, even if she had just saved him from the wrath of the Mediran king. Then her stomach gave a growl, and she grudgingly reached for the bread. The comforting smell wafted over her, and she took a bite before she could think better of it. It was soft and buttery on her tongue, and still warm.

He reached inside the pack again and pulled out another slice of bread, tearing off a chunk and putting it in his mouth. He closed his eyes, and Isabel remembered with a sudden heaviness that this was the best food he'd had in weeks.

Questions tumbled through her mind. He was still here, after all that. He hadn't just left her and made a run for it. He could have. Easily. She'd gotten him out, sure, but he didn't owe her anything. Not after the way he'd been treated, even if she weren't Mediran.

And then there was the torrent of power and shadow that had rushed through her just before she'd passed out, the shadow that had poured out of her and turned day into chaos and night—everything except for her and Karim. They'd erupted out, away from the soldiers, as if there were nothing in their way. A hollowness settled in the pit of her stomach, and the old things the village women had whispered about her came roaring back: *She's a monster. Anyone who can control shadows can't be trusted. There's no telling what she'll do.*

Isabel rubbed a hand across her face. "How long was I asleep?" she asked. It was the only thing she could get her brain to hook on to.

"A few hours. Three at most."

Her heart gave a startled thud. Three hours she'd been at this man's mercy, and he'd given her a blanket? Surely the Medirans couldn't be far behind. "Okay." She bit her lip, her mind working. "Where are we?"

"I was hoping you would know."

"What do you mean?" she said, lowering the bread to her lap.

"I don't know this land at all." He shrugged. "It's your territory. Or rather, I assume it is, since I still know nothing about you."

"We can't be far from the Mediran palace," Isabel insisted, ignoring his pointed suggestion. "Maybe a bit to the south, where the forest starts."

He was already shaking his head. "I don't think so. I . . . scouted around a bit. There's no sign of the palace or of the Mediran capital."

She stared at him. That made no sense. They'd been behind the palace before she'd collapsed. All she'd done was get them out. "And where did you get all this again?" She held up the piece of bread.

His mouth quirked. "I thought you said you didn't want to know."

"I don't," she muttered. If they weren't near the Mediran palace, then where were they? He had to have missed something. Something obvious.

She pulled the checkered blanket back up over her legs, thankful for its warmth in the cold evening air.

"I'll have you know I found it somewhere it wasn't likely to be missed," Karim said, his eyes flickering to the quilt over her knees, as if he could read her mind.

"I feel so much better about it now, thanks," she drawled.

"I'm not a thief."

"Then what do you call this?" She held up the bread.

"Payment," he said. "For damages owed."

"So, you know exactly what you deserve then, do you?"

He glared at her, and her mind flashed back to the throne room, to an image of him facing the king in a display of defiance. Her stomach soured. Even he hadn't deserved that.

"What in the name of the archer were you thinking anyway?" she rounded on him. "Mocking the Mediran king? Attacking a guard in the middle of the bloody throne room? Were you trying to get yourself killed?"

Karim gave a bleak laugh. "Did it really matter? They were going to kill me no matter what I did."

She couldn't argue with that. "So, you decided to take on the entire Archer-forsaken Mediran army single handedly?"

"Better to go out in a blaze of glory than let them dictate your death," he said bitterly.

Her heart gave a sudden thump as she stared at him. She hated to admit how much that made sense. After all, it's what she had done, and it had led to her position with the queen's shadow now. "And how did that work out for you?" she asked.

"I'm here, aren't I?"

She gave him an incredulous stare. He *was* here. With her. Somewhere in a forest that couldn't be far from the Mediran palace, with what was probably the entire king's army out looking for them. She suddenly felt more tired than she had before.

He shifted into a sitting position. "I still don't know who you are."

"Isabel Algerin," she said begrudgingly. She didn't like the idea of giving up her name so easily. But her orders had been to rescue him. Rendra needed him to give them answers.

"Karim Saad of Clan Marek."

Clan Marek. She didn't know much about the powerful families of Ineti, but she had heard of Clan Marek. They held power in a part of the empire directly north across the sea from Medira.

"And you're Rendran," he said pointedly.

Isabel nodded. "I work for the Rendran queen. And Rendra needs you in one piece, especially after what happened in the dungeon. You're our one remaining source of information on what the chanters are planning."

"Can't let a valuable resource go to waste," he said bitterly.

"No," she snapped. "I won't let anyone treat another human being like that, no matter what they've done."

He held her gaze for a moment. "And what is it you think I've done?"

She opened her mouth, then stopped. Suddenly, she wasn't sure of what she'd thought she'd known about the Inetian traitors. She'd lumped them all under an umbrella of stupidity, of people who couldn't see beyond their own huge noses. People who are motivated only by power and wealth at the expense of everyone else. But now, with him sitting here in front of her, she wasn't sure at all anymore.

"All I know is that something drove you to join Sethos Amanakar's plan to depose his father from the Inetian throne. And your friends back there seemed willing to risk the end of the world just for more *power—*"

"*Don't,*" Karim barked. His eyes blazed wildly beneath his tangled black hair. "You know absolutely nothing about that."

Well. She had clearly hit a nerve. "You're right," she said slowly, sitting back. "I don't."

His shoulders relaxed slightly. "The Inetian emperor is not just. He uses people for his own gain. My family was cast out by the emperor because my uncle accidentally embarrassed him. The emperor ruined the lives of dozens for the sake of his own vanity. For better or worse, I made a choice to join Amanakar. And it landed me here." His voice was hard. "And what I said to the king was correct. I want nothing to do with the Sorothi chanters ever again."

"And why not?" she pressed. "What did they do to you, Karim?"

He dropped his gaze. "They killed my brother."

The world sharpened at his words, narrowing to a single point. Her heart gave a painful thump, and for a moment, she was back in that room so long ago, watching a pair of gray eyes stare glassily up at her, feeling an overly hot, limp hand clutching her own, hearing a voice begging her for help.

Karim stared out into the forest, his face eerily still. "Akil didn't have the magic affinity that I did. He struggled to control his chant. I tried my best to help him but . . . " He shook his head. "He lost control. He was the one who tore the rift in the fabric of the world back in the enclave. It sucked him in. He was gone. Just like that. And there was nothing I could do."

Isabel remembered Cassandra's story of the explosion at the enclave, of the horrible wrongness that had permeated the valley. To be sucked into such a rift was a fate worse than death, tangled forever in the fabric of the world, neither in earth nor shadow.

"I'm sorry," she said softly.

When he looked up, his black eyes blazed with rage and purpose. "The whole thing was a bad idea from the very beginning. But neither of us had a choice. That's why I haven't run. If your queen is even a single iota smarter than that self-absorbed sop back in Medira, then I'm willing to help in any way I can." His mouth tipped sardonically. "Besides, I'm not stupid. The protection of another crown is the only way I'll survive for more than ten minutes out here."

He wasn't wrong. He could run, but he was wanted in Medira, Rendra, and Ineti. His best bet was to flee south into the Alliance lands, but there were bounty hunters who were willing to do just about anything to claim a reward.

Karim's mouth twisted. "And the man who rescued the others from the dungeon . . . Well, let's just say that he won't be too happy to find out that I didn't come when he called."

"So, it was one of the chanters then," Isabel said.

Karim nodded. "Yes. His name is Gustav. He's the one who brokered the deal with Amanakar. He has an . . . interest in keeping us under his thumb."

Isabel's brows rose. "And why is that?"

His mouth tipped. "I think I'll keep that information to myself until I've got a deal for protection in hand."

Isabel narrowed her eyes, meeting him stare-for-stare. "Well then," she said. "I can say for certain that the Rendran queen is nothing like the Mediran king."

"Good." His eyes slid down to the knife at her belt. "The woman who gave that to you. Who is she?"

Isabel's hand went protectively to the dagger. "Her name is Cassandra. The Rendran queen's shadow, and the queen's half-sister."

Karim blinked, and Isabel could see the cogs turning in his mind. "No wonder she didn't want her identity revealed," he said.

Dots were connecting in Isabel's mind now too. Cassandra and her now-husband Arphaxad had been apprehended by the Inetians in the enclave and then entombed with the rift Karim's brother had been sucked into in an attempt to dispose of them.

"So, she survived then," Karim said slowly.

"She did," Isabel said

"How?" he pressed. "I was there, in the cave. The earth was coming down around us and the chanters had forced her and the man with her to stay by the rift. I used that knife to sever the ropes around their wrists. To give them a fighting chance." His fingers flexed. "I had hoped that the wards in the knife might give them some sort of protection."

He had helped Cassandra? Isabel watched him for a long moment, her mind spinning. A traitor to his country, but still filled with so much conviction of right and wrong.

She told him briefly of Cassandra and Arphaxad's escape, about how they'd found one of the enclave's enchanted doors, gateways that led from one place to another, sometimes hundreds of miles apart.

"So, you gave her this dagger," she said, pulling it out and laying it across her knees.

Karim nodded. His eyes darted from the knife up to hers. "And she gave it to you."

A shiver moved through Isabel at his words. A strange sequence of events, of coincidence, that had led them here to this place, in a cold, quiet forest beneath a silent, gray sky.

Isabel ran her fingers along the hilt, the wards twining up her fingers, a warm, familiar comfort by now. "I don't think she knew about the wards in it."

Karim's mouth tipped. "But you do."

She couldn't stop the answering half-smile that rose to her lips. "I could sense them from a mile away. They're not exactly subtle."

"Wards don't need to be subtle. Not many notice the magic that's been worked around them."

"So, they *are* your wards then." It wasn't a question so much as a statement. She didn't know exactly how wards like these worked, but she knew those with the magic to work them were exceedingly rare.

"They are." He grinned, his eyes flashing mischievously. "You haven't noticed yet, have you?"

"What?"

All at once, she saw them. Wards, sequestering the space around them. They hovered in the air, crackling between the bare branches of the trees, a haze of magic meant to misdirect, to hide their makeshift camp from any prying eyes. She shook her head. He was good. Very good. "That's . . . that's impressive."

He smirked. "I know."

"So, your affinity somehow made you able to see through my magic?"

"I think so," Karim said. "I'm not actually sure *why* though. And what you did this afternoon with shadow—I've never seen anything like it."

Isabel shifted beneath his gaze. “That was different,” she said a little too quickly. “That’s never happened to me before.”

His brows rose. “It hasn’t?”

“No,” she said. “My affinity has always allowed me to . . . disappear into the shadows. Misdirect the eye in the right conditions, especially in darkness. But today I . . . I have no idea what happened. How I did that.”

“Interesting,” he said thoughtfully.

“It doesn’t matter.” She didn’t want to talk about it, especially not with him.

“But it does matter,” he said. “The way our magic works, the way magic is *supposed* to work, is for those with affinities to coax elements of our world to be *more* of what they already are. You draw on shadows—shadows that already exist. You just coax them to be what they’ve wanted to be all along; you convince them that you are a part of them.”

Isabel’s brows drew together. She’d never heard magic described in that way before. She’d spent a lot of her life pretending her affinity didn’t exist, pretending she wasn’t the monster the villagers had claimed she was. Until she had come to work for Cassandra—then her ability to hide in shadows had proven incredibly useful. But she’d never told anyone about it.

"I'm able to weave strands of magic into physical items—into anything that has a physical form really," Karim continued. "This magic coaxes the item to be more of what it was already meant to be. So, the wards around us now—I've simply encouraged the trees to be trees and the forest to be forest. That they exist more intensely than we do. And it hides us."

Isabel sat back, her mind doing its best to catch up with what he was saying.

His lips pressed together. "But the Sorothi chanters—they use words and power to force the world around them into doing something it doesn't want to, into being something it's not. Those doors they tear in the fabric of the world should not be able to exist. It's an unnatural kind of magic, one in which humans impose their own will on the earth rather than working within the bounds of what things are supposed to be." His fingers clenched. "It's another reason I want nothing more to do with the chanters and their magic."

Nothing more to do with the chanters and their magic. She understood now how important it was to get him back to Rendra. The information he carried was going to be indispensable to finding the chanters, to stopping whatever they planned to do with their unnatural magic.

"So," she said slowly. "You're telling me that my job is to get the most wanted man in Ineti and Medira back to Rendra without tearing apart a newly budding alliance between my nation and the one I just sprung you out of."

His mouth curved. "Sounds fun."

She pushed herself to her feet, saving the checkered blanket from dropping into the mud. "You have a warped sense of fun."

"Considering my idea of fun for the past few weeks involved not starving to death, I'll take this version any day."

Another twinge of guilt twisted in her gut. "So, we agree that we need to get you to Rendra then?" she said.

"Yep," he tossed back.

"Okay," she said. "Let's get going. We still need to figure out where we are." But even as the words left her mouth, she had a hunch—a terrifying hunch—that she knew exactly where they were.

Karim folded the checkered blanket and put it in the pack along with the food before shouldering it. Isabel slid the knife back in her belt, strangely comforted by its presence. Karim whispered something under his breath and flicked his fingers, and the wards came down. Isabel watched, impressed. She'd never seen anyone do anything like that before. She was used to being the only one with a magic affinity.

Karim followed her through the trees. It didn't take long to realize that they were heading toward the top of a ridge. Ahead, the trees parted to reveal streaks of orange angling through the clouds. If they could get to the top, they might be able to figure out how far from the Mediran palace they were.

Her heart pounded as they moved through the trees, reaching for the openness on the other side of the crest. Her sinking suspicion was already proving to be far too likely.

They burst through the trees at the top of the rise. The setting sun was just piercing through the gray cloud cover, sending tendrils of gold and blue brilliantly across the horizon. In the far distance, Isabel could see the faint shimmer of the ocean. Below them, a river snaked in shining hues across the fields of cold-weather crops. She could see the outline of another river to the east.

There, nestled in a pristine valley where the two rivers met, was a plethora of man-made structures, pushing along the riverbanks and up around a hill. On the high ground was a glittering palace, at once familiar and terrifying. Isabel's stomach did a flip.

They weren't in Medira at all. They were staring down at the capital city of Rendra and the glittering facade of the Rendran palace. A chill crept across her body. They were a hundred miles from where they had started only a few hours before. And Isabel had no idea how.

Chapter 4

Isabel shifted awkwardly at the back of the study in the Rendran palace, her eyes on the figure of the queen a few feet in front of her.

The queen was dressed in a simple blue gown edged with silver thread, and her dark, graying hair was pulled sharply back from her face. Isabel had only seen the queen from a distance before, but now, up close, she could make out the lines around her eyes and mouth that denoted a deep weariness.

The sun had set by the time they'd made their way into the city, and under the cover of darkness, Isabel had been able to pull enough shadow to cover both her and Karim. There had been no time to think about how they'd traveled across half of Medira and into Rendra. No time to let herself dwell on the terrifying implications of it all.

They'd located Cassandra quickly within the palace. The queen's shadow had given Karim one measured glance before ushering them into the study they now sat in, with its blue and gold wallpaper. Then she'd covertly sent for the queen.

Now Karim sat on a gold embroidered chair not far from Isabel, looking just as grimy and wild as she was sure she looked.

Cassandra perched on a plush divan beside her sister. For the first time, Isabel realized how much the two women looked alike. Cassandra, almost twenty years younger, was a stronger, slimmer version of the queen. They both boasted high cheekbones, aquiline noses, and thick, dark hair, though Cassandra's was done in a more casual knot than the queen's.

"So, from what I understand, you are Karim Saad, and you were part of Amanakar's plot," the queen said. She watched Karim with a piercing intensity, as if she could see straight through him. To his credit, Karim didn't allow his gaze to drop from the queen's, and Isabel hoped he wouldn't do something as incredibly stupid as the stunt he'd pulled in Medira. "You're willing to give Rendra information in order to apprehend your countrymen and bring the rogue chanters to justice."

Isabel had given a brief account of what had happened in the dungeons of Medira, of the king's anger at Karim, of her rash act of saving him. She'd glossed over the strangeness of her shadow magic and how they'd gone from Media to Rendra in a matter of minutes. How the power had rushed out of her and left her in an exhausted heap on the forest floor. How Karim had set up wards to protect them while she slept. None of that was the queen's concern.

"I am," Karim said after a stretch of silence. "In exchange for the queen's protection."

The queen folded her hands firmly in her lap, then traded a glance with Cassandra. "That can be arranged," she said.

Karim blinked. "I— Oh. Thank you, Your Royal Highness."

"Easier than you expected?" Cassandra asked with a grin.

"After what happened in Medira? Yes." Karim rubbed the back of his head sheepishly.

"I am not in the business of hurting those who wish for my help," the queen said.

A swell of pride moved through Isabel's chest. At least one sovereign wasn't self-serving. It was what had made her want to work for the queen. What had made her want to serve her country. Because she knew the queen truly wanted things to be better for her subjects.

"Besides." Cassandra leaned forward. "I need to thank you for what you did for my husband and me at the enclave. If it weren't for you, I don't know that we would have made it out alive."

"I *am* glad you made it out," Karim said earnestly. "On behalf of my people, I'm truly sorry. I should have done something sooner."

"But you did act," Cassandra said, "when no one else did."

The door opened, and a man around Cassandra's age stepped into the study. He was clean shaven, with a slim waist and broad shoulders. Dark, curling hair shaded brown eyes that twinkled with mischief. His gaze traveled across the group assembled in the room. When it landed on Cassandra, his face visibly softened.

"Arphaxad," the queen said. "I'm glad you could join us.

Arphaxad Ilin Serra, Cassandra's husband and the nephew of the king of Medira, gave a quick bow to the queen. Tension eased out of Cassandra's shoulders as her husband slid onto the divan beside her. He ran a hand lightly across the small of her back, and she smiled up at him.

"Sorry." He leaned forward so his arms rested on his knees. "I only just received word that my attendance was required. And thank goodness, because you saved me from a mountain of intensely boring paperwork." His gaze settled on Karim, and he blinked. "Wait. Do I know you from somewhere?"

"I'm surprised you remember at all, dear," Cassandra said. "You were a bit incapacitated at the time."

Arphaxad cast a glance at his wife, then suddenly his eyes widened. "The knife," he said, looking at Karim. "In the cave. You freed us."

Isabel's fingers went unconsciously to the knife at her belt. The wards radiated warmth into her fingers as Karim gave a quick nod of acquiescence.

"And *how* did he come to be here?" Arphaxad asked. After Cassandra filled him in, he shook his head. "That's all . . . very concerning."

Isabel thought it was a little more than concerning.

"It *is* concerning," Cassandra said, leaning back against the divan. "What I want to know is why? Why go to all that trouble to free those men?"

Karim sighed, running a hand absently through his hair. The action made it stick up more than it already did. "I don't know the whole of it," he said. "We weren't told much when we were in Medira. But it seems that Gustav escaped the raid in which most of us were captured."

Cassandra's hands balled into fists. "I swear, if I ever see that man again, I'm going to rip his head from his shoulders before he realizes what's happening."

"Not if I get to him first," Arphaxad said.

The queen raised her hand. "I presume this Gustav had something to do with the escape?"

Karim nodded. "Yes. He is the most powerful of the ruling chanters in the enclave. He was able to shatter the old wards around the dungeon and open doors to get the other men out."

"He broke through the old wards?" Arphaxad whistled. "That's— I thought that was impossible."

"I did too," Karim said. "We all did."

Cassandra shook her head. "How did he do it?"

"I really don't know." Karim's shoulders tensed as he spoke. "I was only in the enclave for two months. We'd barely begun to scratch the surface of what the chanters know." He let out a slow breath then, suddenly looking very tired. "But he's jaded. Jaded about the enclave's position. Jaded that their magic is seen as dangerous."

"Even though it is," Cassandra muttered.

"Yes." There was a chill in Karim's voice. "He wants something better for the enclave. More power. More recognition for their work. It was part of why he made the deal with Amanakar."

"And what was it that he was promised in return?" Cassandra asked. "That is what I've never fully been able to parse out. The remaining chanters in the enclave have been . . . cagey at best."

"Amanakar promised Gustav access to Ineti's old libraries, where there are texts of deep magic detailing workings that have been lost to time. They're mostly under the protection of the emperor and of powerful wards. And if Gustav helped Amanakar overthrow the emperor, he would be able to give him access to them."

Isabel shuddered. There had once been texts of old magic in Rendra and Medira too, but they'd been hidden or destroyed years ago.

"What does he plan to do with access to these old texts?" Cassandra asked quietly. Arphaxad's shoulders were hunched, and the queen watched Karim with a solemn expression.

"He wants to bring the magic of the old mages back into our world. And the only way to do that is to reforge a path into the realm of shadow."

Cassandra swore under her breath. Arphaxad slammed a fist down onto the divan, and the queen turned pale. Isabel gaped at Karim. Reforge a path into shadow. That was . . . madness. The old mages had derived their power from the ancient gates between their world and the shadow realm, but those links had been closed five hundred years ago for a reason. The more power the mages had drawn, the more shadow had slipped through—shadow that was hungry to devour life. Shadow that had taken a ring of the most powerful mages the world had seen to quell.

"That's why Gustav wanted to free us," Karim said quietly. "He is powerful, but he can't do everything he wants alone. Chanting, especially, takes a lot of power, and to create the type of doors the enclave was capable of takes years of study and multiple powerful chanters. Now that Gustav's been rejected by the enclave and is on the run, those of us in the prison are his best chance of gathering chanters to help him. Now that he's freed them, they owe him their lives. That's a powerful incentive for wanted men." Karim's mouth twisted.

"But not for you," the queen said.

"Not for me," Karim said.

"Do you know where they went?" Cassandra asked. Her eyes were blazing now, and Isabel could see the cogs turning in her head. There was a reason she was the queen's shadow—she always had a plan.

"I think it's likely they went to the Alliance lands," Karim said. "At least for now. Gustav is from the southern reaches, near the ice sheets."

"Well out of our reach," Arphaxad said with a sigh.

"I'll put out some feelers," Cassandra said. "We have contacts in the Alliance lands. We want to keep as close an eye on him as possible."

The queen turned her gaze on Karim. "You said you do not want to have anything to do with the chanters again. You refused to go when the chanters came for your men. Does that mean you've drawn a target on your back? You have information they don't want known."

Karim stared down at his hands. "I think it is likely that they will try to come for me," he said slowly. Isabel wondered how much that might have to do with his magic affinity over any information he might have. He was powerful—she'd seen that firsthand. Gustav must know that too.

"I see," the queen said. Then, "He can't stay here for long."

"No, he can't," Cassandra agreed. "You have a target too firmly on your back—from Medira, from Ineti, and from Gustav. And if Medira finds out that one of our own broke you out—I don't want to know what it will mean for the alliance between Rendra and Medira." Her hand found her husband's and gave it a quick squeeze.

Karim sat rigidly in his chair, his shoulders stiff. Isabel's heart ached suddenly as she looked at him. He was alone in a foreign land, unable to return home to his family, to the familiar places he had once known. And not only that, but the land that had once been his had turned against him. It seemed incredibly unfair.

"There's a safe house of sorts at the base of the southern mountains, just north of the Alliance lands," Cassandra continued. "It's remote—an ancient Rendran citadel, protected by old wards. The protector who lives there is as loyal to the queen as they come. He can go there for the time being. Until things settle down."

Until things settle down. That could take months. Years even. But the queen was right that he couldn't stay in the palace where there were too many prying eyes. The Mediran ambassador to Rendra was a sharp man. Word would make its way back to the king in time.

"Is that amenable to you, Mr. Saad?" the queen asked.

Karim crossed his arms. "It's better than some of my other options."

"Good." The queen cast her gaze around the room then. "Now, as for the matter of who will accompany Mr. Saad—"

"I can take him," Isabel said, straightening from where she was leaning against the wall.

All eyes in the room turned toward her. She winced. Damn it. She had just interrupted *the queen.*

"I feel responsible for him," she blundered on. "I was the one who broke him out and got him in this predicament. It's my responsibility to see it through to the end."

And there weren't any better candidates anyway. Cassandra was too tied up in the capital for a job like this—since her marriage to Arphaxad and the revelation that she was the queen's half-sister, she was far too visible. Isabel had taken over the brunt of Cassandra's old activities in the past few months. This would just be one more.

"I see," the queen said slowly.

Karim had turned around in his chair and was watching her, an unreadable expression on his face.

"It makes sense to me," Arphaxad said. He cast a glance at his wife. "Cass?"

"Isabel is more than capable of taking care of this," Cassandra said, giving Isabel a warm smile. "Though I do miss galivanting through Rendra on my own."

"You forget, you have me now, dear," Arphaxad said, draping an arm around her shoulders. Cassandra rolled her eyes, but gave his hand a fond pat.

"Good," the queen said, looking between Isabel and Karim. "We will find a place for Mr. Saad to rest tonight. You will both leave in the morning." She shot an unexpectedly impish smile at her younger sister. "And if my understanding of how Isabel came to work for Cassandra is correct, I don't doubt her ability at all."

Isabel's cheeks flooded with heat. The queen knew *that* story? Her heart gave a panicked thump. The *queen* knew that story.

Cassandra groaned. "We are not talking about that, Elena."

"Um, we most certainly are going to talk about that." Arphaxad pulled his wife playfully against him. "I don't believe I've heard this particular story."

Cassandra put her hands over her cheeks. "No, no, no, we are *not* talking about that."

Isabel couldn't help the smile that tugged at her lips. It *was* a good story. And maybe not her proudest moment. Or maybe it was. She'd never been able to decide. She'd been in a place of desperation, and then she'd seen Cassandra and . . . it had all fallen stupidly into place.

"It's Isabel's story to tell!" Cassandra protested, pressing her hands to her cheeks.

Arphaxad turned to look at Isabel, a pleading, almost puppy-dog look on his face.

"I don't mind," Isabel said with a grin.

Karim shot her a look, his eyes gleaming with interest. Isabel's cheeks flamed, and she yanked her gaze away.

"As I understand it," the queen said, leaning forward, "Isabel beat Cassandra at her own game. She successfully captured and incapacitated the queen's shadow *with a bucket of dirty dishwater*. And then she asked for a job."

Isabel didn't think it was possible for her face to turn even redder than it already was. She had been desperate for something, anything, to change in her life, to find a place that didn't come with the memories of what she'd lost. There wasn't much in the Rendran capital for a girl from a small farming village with no family and no references. But so much of it had been chance—that she'd happened to see Cassandra in that alley behind the courtier's residence in which she worked, that she'd recognized her at all, that she happened to be holding that enormous bucket of dishwater . . .

"I was a little distracted that day," Cassandra protested.

Arphaxad laughed gleefully. "That is incredible," he said to Isabel. "I pulled that kind of thing off a few times when I was still working for Medira, but I have heard of no one else who has. I am honored to have you join my ranks."

"You are insufferable." Cassandra punched her husband in the arm, but she was grinning too.

Isabel crossed her arms, trying to keep her smile at bay. She couldn't stop herself from glancing back at Karim. He grinned, and her cheeks flooded with heat again.

"Well then," the queen said, rising. Cassandra and Arphaxad rose too, with Karim following suit a moment later. "I believe we have a plan in place."

"Yes, we do," Cassandra confirmed.

"Isabel will show you to your accommodations," the queen said to Karim. "If you will excuse me, I have another matter to attend to."

"Of course, Your Highness," Karim said with a bow. He seemed far more in awe of the Rendran queen than he had been of the Mediran king.

Cassandra gave Isabel directions to a room at the back of the palace, a room that had old wards on it.

"Thank you, Isabel," Cassandra said, reaching for her arm. "I don't know what I would do without you." Isabel's heart warmed for a moment, and she gave the older woman a quick nod before following Karim out into the hall.

"Interesting," Karim said when they were alone.

"What's interesting?" Isabel said thornily, her shoulders tensing. She didn't like that introspective look at all. It meant he was about to question something she'd done.

He shrugged. "You didn't tell them. About the shadow. About what happened back in Medira. How we got here."

"*I* don't even know what happened," she said defensively. "It's not something they need to know. It's not relevant to what's going on now."

Karim's brows rose. "They don't know about your affinity, do they?"

"It's not something I'm exactly interested in publicizing," Isabel said tightly. The fact that he hadn't said anything to them was more than she had expected. But she supposed he'd had no reason to reveal her secrets. He had no reason to reveal his own either.

"You didn't tell them about mine either," he said.

"Did you want them knowing about your affinity?" she asked. "I fully believe in the Rendran queen. She has been nothing but good to me. But even a good sovereign must use the tools they have. I don't think you want that added layer of usefulness to them."

He looked at her for a long moment, his eyes pensive, assessing. She didn't like him looking at her like that, as if he were truly considering what she'd said. She'd rather he'd just snap at her and give her a reason to go on disliking him.

She had stopped thinking of him as a traitor, Isabel realized suddenly, which made her want to stomp her foot. It would have been so much easier to just go on that way.

"Look," she said, letting out a puff of air. "If we're going to work together, you can't question me. It's my job to get you to the citadel. It's your job to follow. Got that?"

Karim raised his hands in a gesture of surrender. "As my lady commands."

Isabel tossed him her most scathing glare but didn't bother giving him the satisfaction of a response.

They had a long journey ahead of them. It was time to get some rest. And Isabel knew they both needed it.

Chapter 5

They left before dawn.

Isabel had knocked on Karim's door with sleep still dragging at her eyes, a light pack strapped to her back. They needed to get an early start. It was going to be a grueling, six-day journey to the citadel, even with the help of Cassandra's extensive network.

Karim had emerged from his room looking just as tired as she felt. He'd clearly taken a bath and cleaned the grime from his face and hair. The stolen coat was gone, replaced with a well-fitting leather tunic that punctuated his dark hair and bronze skin. His face was still purple and bruised, but the swelling had gone down considerably, and he'd shaved the ragged beard. She'd blinked. She hadn't thought very hard about what he looked like before, but with the grime cleaned from his face, wearing clothes that fit him well, he was . . . better looking than she'd expected.

"Are you ready?" she'd asked a little too curtly, surveying the pack he'd slung over his back, outfitted, as she'd been, by Cassandra.

"I'd have preferred to sleep for a few more days," he said. "But sure."

Isabel would have too, but she couldn't let him know that. "There will be plenty of time for you to sleep when you're dead."

"I *would* be dead by now if it weren't for you."

She arched a brow at him. "Well, you will be dead soon if we don't get moving."

He followed her through the quiet halls of the pre-dawn palace and into the empty streets of the Rendran capital. Most of the inhabitants hadn't woken up yet, and only a few carts trundled through the cobblestone streets, lanterns of enchanted orb fire hung on poles above their seats. A few people hurried through the alleys, some with packs slung over their backs, others leading animals or swigging from a final pint of ale. Isabel knew the streets would be bustling before long as the sun pushed its way over the horizon, full of hawkers shouting their wares, mothers with their children going to market, and dogs yapping at people's heels.

When Isabel had first arrived in the capital four years earlier—a fresh farm girl from the north—she had been at once overwhelmed and delighted by the frenzy of the city. It was a place that was easy to disappear into, a place where one could become anonymous, forgotten, left to do as they pleased. A place where she could use her magic without people giving her suspicious glares and whispering about dealings with darkness.

It was also the place that had taken everything from her.

The densely gathered villas of the city gave way to smaller, less opulent structures, and then those faded into clay-roof houses with spacious gardens. The fields beyond that were green with cold-weather crops—cabbage, lettuce, and rutabaga pushing their way through the damp earth.

Isabel's body ached from the ordeal the day before, and she could tell Karim was just as exhausted. After weeks locked up in a tiny cell with minimal food, he was weak. Guilt tugged at her chest. Maybe she *should* have let him rest for another day or two.

They came to a squat stable at the outskirts of the city, and Isabel showed the sign of the queen's shadow to the proprietor. A few minutes later they were outfitted with a pair of brown mares, one with a white diamond on her forehead, and the other with a white muzzle. Isabel pulled herself onto the one with the white muzzle.

"You can ride, right?" she asked Karim.

"Of course," he said curtly. "I was in the military. Cavalry." He held out his hand for the horse to sniff, then patted her neck, his fingers slow and sure. The horse's ears flicked back in interest, and then she turned and nuzzled Karim's hand with her nose.

Karim smiled. It was the first genuine smile she'd seen from him, untinged by bitterness, since this whole sorry business had started.

She hardly knew anything about him, she realized, watching as he moved around to the horse's side and expertly pulled himself into the saddle. What *had* his life had been like back in Ineti—before his family's fall from grace, before he'd been sent on Amankar's doomed mission to Medira?

Karim looked up at her then, his eyes bright, and she jerked her gaze away. She didn't need to be thinking thoughts like that. It was enough to know that he was human, that he deserved some semblance of respect—even if he were a complicated sort of traitor.

"I don't suppose you could try that trick with your magic again and just carry us where we need to go," Karim said dryly as they guided their horses out into the road.

"I don't suppose you could find your own way to the citadel to save me the trouble," Isabel returned. "I'm not going to risk my hide just to save you from a few measly miles of travel."

Karim's lips twitched. "I suppose I'll learn to endure."

"You better," she said as she nudged her horse into a canter.

He was right that he could ride. He kept his seat as if he were part of the horse, his hands sure on the reins, whereas Isabel, who had ridden mostly plodding farm horses until she'd started working for Cassandra, sat like a sack of potatoes next to him.

They followed the main road south until the farm fields gave way to thickening rows of trees, then turned along a smaller lane to the southwest as the forest thickened, trees sprouting almost impossibly high into the crisp autumn air. They stopped a few times to eat, to stretch, and to water their horses, and each time, Isabel couldn't help but watch the quiet wood around them for signs of movement. Just because nothing unusual had happened so far didn't mean they were safe.

"Gustav is good, but he's not that good," Karim said when she glanced over her shoulder for the fiftieth time that afternoon. "Chanting is a precise business. They would have to locate us first and then understand how to open a door to where we are. And we've been constantly on the move. I'd say we have at least a few days' lead time."

Somehow, that didn't make Isabel feel any better.

Each day they moved, the snow-capped mountains in the south—their destination—inched a little closer. There, on a rocky cliffside that wasn't marked on any map, was the old citadel, secured by wards that kept those who had no business there from finding it.

At night, they stumbled, exhausted and bone-weary, into one roadside inn or safe house or another, owned by one of Cassandra's contacts.

"We'll have to leave our horses here," Isabel said to Karim the evening of the third night as they dismounted in front of a small inn near the foot of the mountains. "The path climbs sharply from here—at least where we're going."

The tavern was small but glowing with light. Isabel had met Marta, the owner, a few times. She was a round, smiling woman with two teenage sons, but Isabel knew there was a will of iron beneath her soft exterior. She had worked for Andre, the queen's shadow before Cassandra, and had proven her loyalty to the crown more than once.

"How many rooms?" Marta asked when Isabel showed her the sign of the queen's shadow, her eyes darting curiously between Isabel and Karim.

"Two, please," Isabel said a little too quickly, her cheeks flooding with heat. Karim snorted beside her as Marta raised a suggestive brow at them.

That night, Isabel fell onto the straw tick bed (in her *own* room) and slept like the dead.

Karim was already up and shoveling down a bowl of grits and bacon when Isabel came down the next morning.

"Here," he said, tossing a leather object in her direction. Isabel caught it and held it up. It was a sheath for a dagger, the black leather marked and worn, and she could feel the wards twining through it—safety, strength, precision, alertness.

She gaped at him. "When did you have the time to make this?"

"Last night." His eyes flashed with mischief. "And since I had my *own* room, I had the time."

She gave him an indignant look. Her stomach clenched as she looked at the sheath. "I can't take this, Karim. You'll need it, probably more than I do."

"Oh, I have warded pieces of my own, don't worry about that." He patted the belt around his waist with its knives. "But since you have my dagger—I figured it needed a home."

She swallowed, her fingers curling around the sheath. It was an incredible piece of work. Despite his blasé demeanor, this wasn't something he had just tossed together. He was incredibly skilled. She had known that already, but seeing this, knowing he had spent so much time and energy for *her*—her heart clenched.

"Thank you," she said roughly, hating the wobble in her voice. She couldn't remember the last time anyone had done something so specifically for her. Not since her first days in the Rendran capital.

A cold wind was blowing in from the south when they set out, and Isabel pulled the deep hood of her cloak over her head to stave it off. She watched quietly as Karim said goodbye to his horse, running his fingers gently along the mare's flank.

"Let's go," he said, giving the mare a final pat.

The way was flat at first, winding into the trees, but steepened sharply. Isabel could feel it in her legs as the day wore on. Karim was getting slower, and she tried not to think of the weeks he'd spent in the darkness of the Mediran dungeon. He'd gotten stronger even in the days they'd been traveling, but she knew his body hadn't had enough time to heal.

The path flattened out again around midday as they reached the top of a rise. The trees were thick and dark around them, and they stopped by a narrow stream, fed by the snowmelt from the mountains higher up. Isabel pulled her pack off and rolled her shoulders to release the tension that had built there.

Karim removed his water skin from his pack, then wordlessly reached for hers, filling both before handing hers back. As Isabel took a long swig, she realized how used to him she'd gotten in the past few days. How much of a rhythm they'd fallen into. A sinking feeling gathered in her gut as she straightened. She couldn't afford to think like that. She had been alone for the last three years—she couldn't get used to having another person around. This camaraderie that was building between them wouldn't last. Couldn't last.

Karim eased his pack back on, then stilled beside her, his brows drawn together as he peered downstream.

A flock of blackbirds startled into the air, and Isabel's hands dropped to her sides as she watched them. The back of her neck prickled, and a rolling sense of dread washed over her.

Karim frowned. "Something doesn't feel right about—"

A flash seared the riverbed, like a bolt of lightning striking too close, and the acrid scent of sulfur rent the air. Isabel dropped to the ground, throwing one hand over her head, while the other yanked Karim's knife out of her belt.

The wards reacted, threading up her arm in a hiss of power until her body was tingling with warmth.

There was a shout, followed by words Isabel didn't understand. Her body went cold. She was hearing Inetian. How had Gustav's men found them?

Six men materialized out of the brush along the river, dressed in grays and greens and browns, swords glinting in the sunlight that filtered through the trees. Karim stood at her back now, his own daggers in his hands, and she could sense the coiled tension radiating from him. She desperately tried to gather shadow around them, but even with the help of the wards in the knife and its sheath, the shadows were too thin, too fragile in the daylight to do much more than flicker around her ankles before dissipating all together.

"I see you're still doing Gustav's dirty work, Paarsav," Karim said from behind her.

The man closest to them pressed his lips together, and Isabel could see his grip on the short sword in his hand tighten. He was broad-shouldered, with golden brown skin and a wicked-looking scar that traveled from his left temple and across his cheek. He was maybe twenty years older than Isabel, but there was a hollowness to his cheeks that spoke of his weeks in the Mediran prison.

"Just come with us, Karim," the man said tiredly. "You should have left when the doors first opened in the prison. Instead, we've had to spend precious time and energy searching for you."

Karim tensed. "You shouldn't have bothered."

"You know we need you. You have abilities none of us could ever fathom, even if we spent years learning what Gustav had to teach us."

Isabel remembered the way Karim's wards had twined above them in the forest after they'd escaped the Mediran prison. She could feel the strength and surety of the wards he'd woven into the knife now in her hand. She had no trouble believing that Karim was as powerful as this man claimed, even if Karim downplayed it himself.

"I'm sure Gustav would be more than happy to use me in any way he can," Karim said sarcastically.

Paarsav's eyes narrowed. "So, you're truly deserting your countrymen when we have nothing."

"I'm not deserting you!" Isabel could feel the fury radiating from him. "You were *there*, Paarsav. You *saw* what happened to Akil. Gustav is using you. He's using us all. He needs chanters to help him open doors. And if you mess up—he's not coming to save you, not from a rift."

"He was the only one willing to do anything about us rotting away in that abysmal prison," an angular man to Paarsav's right spat.

"And that suddenly makes what he's trying to do right and just?" Karim drawled. "I know none of you are stupid. If Gustav gets his hands on those texts of old magic, if he amasses enough power to break through into shadow, the entire world will end up like what we sat in the cave—shattered and broken, the edges between earth and shadow blurring. *No one* will be safe, least of all you."

Paarsav's eyes flashed dangerously. "Don't tell me you're innocent of all this, Saad. There's no way you made it this far so quickly without opening doors of your own."

"Believe what you want," Karim said. "But I'm done with Gustav. I'm done with all this."

Paarsav took a step forward. "And where are you going to go? We can protect you. Help you." His mouth twisted bitterly. "Believe me, I understand exactly the predicament you're in. We are all in it too. No land to go back to. Wanted in every corner of the world. We're trying to fix that. Trying to create a space for ourselves."

"And doing an abysmal job of it," Karim said.

"Don't waste any more time talking with a traitor like him," the angular man to Paarsav's right spat.

Traitor? Isabel almost snorted.

"Just kill him now. Be done with it. This world would be far better off without him in it."

Isabel took a step forward. "You'll have to get through me first," she snarled.

The angular man's eyes flicked to her, then traveled down her body in a way that made her want to gouge his eyes out. "Who's the girl?"

"That's none of your business, Ankar," Karim said sharply.

A sly smile spread across Ankar's face, and he said something in Inetian that made Karim bark what Isabel was certain was an obscenity.

"Give it a rest, Ankar." Paarsav cast a tired glance at the man beside him. "I'm giving you one more chance, Saad. Come with us willingly, and there will be no consequences. You're our brother. You belong with us after all we've been through."

"Can't you see that none of it matters?" Karim's voice took on a note of desperation. "We were all being used—by Sethos, by Gustav, by *everyone*. You're better than this! There *is* another way."

"Maybe for you," Paarsav said. "But not for us."

The earth rumbled beneath their feet as the pair of men on the other side of the stream began to chant. Their words twined in the air, crackling with power and magic and meaning.

Ankar charged, his dagger raised, while Paarsav darted forward. Isabel shifted, ready to throw herself to the side and let Ankar's momentum knock him off balance. They could take two of them, maybe three, but not six.

"Isabel!" Karim shouted, and suddenly she felt his fingers wrapped around hers, power crackling in his touch. "Pull your shadow, *now.*"

Isabel did as he asked. Shadow still lingered from when she'd tried pulling it earlier. Before, it had been an intangible thing, somewhere out of her reach, but now, it thundered around her, stripping away from the forest floor and the branches of the trees and the mossy trunks. Power and shadow roared through her limbs until she thought she might burst; it wrapped around them like a torrent, as powerful as the moon and the wind and the night. She let out an involuntary howl at the intensity of it, wanting it all to blow away, for the pressure building in her head and her hands and her arms to release.

And suddenly it did, like an explosion, and shadow howled and raged into the forest, wrapping around the men as they tried to flee, their screams disappearing into the raging black cacophony.

"*Move*!" Karim shouted.

And then they were running, power shifting and crackling where their hands twined together, and Isabel had never felt more alive, more full of energy and life and the will to live. The forest flew by them in a flash of silver trunks and craggy branches and twisted needles. All at once she could see a flock of deer skittering out of their path and the birds in the trees fluttering up into the canopy and the salmon shuttling their way through the icy streams of the mountain heights. For a moment, she wanted to know what it was like to fly, to become a bird and stretch out above the mountains so that everything looked tiny and insignificant below, the petty problems of nations and humans fading away at the majesty of it all.

But Karim was holding her hand, and she heard him shout, "Isabel, stop!" and she realized they had to stop, to let this power go, to dissipate. They were brightness and night at once, and it couldn't continue like this forever. So, she stopped.

They both collapsed in a heap on the forest floor. A sharp wind rustled the thick canopy of pines above them. Her body was heavy—so, impossibly heavy. All she wanted to do was crumple into a ball and sleep until the end of time.

Karim was on his knees beside her, looking as stunned as she felt.

"I did it again," she managed weakly. Her vision was swimming. She wanted to sleep. Needed to sleep.

Karim shook his head, his eyes wide and sparkling with more energy than she thought she would ever have again. "That wasn't you," he said. "That was us. Both of us. Together."

"What?" Isabel slurred as the forest swayed around her.

"Our magic," Karim said. "I didn't understand it when it happened before, but something about the way our magics collide—*this* happens."

"Oh," she said, hardly able to comprehend what he was saying. So, it wasn't her. It was them . . . together. And it was . . . madness. She had never heard of magic of that enormity being worked, not since the time of the old mages.

She laid her head on the ground, despite the chill. "I think . . . I'm going . . . to sleep for a while," she said.

She thought she heard Karim say something, but then her head was swimming, and she drifted out into darkness over a great wide sea. The last thing she remembered was a pair of strong arms wrapping around her, and a voice whispering, "I've got you, Isabel," before everything went dark.

Chapter 6

She woke feeling pleasantly warm. Only the tip of her nose was cold.

A moment passed as she relaxed into the softness and warmth around her, basking in the surety that she was safe.

Her eyes flew open. A bare tree branch was splintered on the ground not far from her face, and mottled leaves glistened with drops of drew.

Memory came to her in bits and flashes—the Inetians confronting them by the riverbed, Karim grabbing her hand, and the shadow that had roared through her, through *them*. Then his dark eyes peering into hers as he caught her when she fell, his sure fingers tucking her into their one remaining bedroll—since she'd left hers by the river with the Inetians—and his warmth as he curled up behind her to stave off the cold so they could both sleep . . .

She shot up and turned a horrified look to the figure beside her. Karim was still curled on his side, his back resting against her hip, his face slack in the peaceful confines of sleep. For a moment, she stared at him. He looked more at peace than she had ever seen him, the hard lines around his mouth and eyes softened to a boyish innocence. She reached out and softly brushed a strand of hair away from his face.

She froze. What in the name of the Archer was she doing?

She yanked her hand back as if she'd been burned, then carefully extracted herself from his bedroll, suddenly furious with herself, with him, with this whole damned situation. Why did he have to be so . . . so concerned for her? It was her duty to get him to the Rendran citadel. All she was doing was her job. The rest of it—her magic, the way he'd tucked her into the bedroll, the dagger and its sheath he'd made specifically for her—didn't matter.

Her head ached, and she sank down onto a half-rotten log to think. A cool breeze whispered through the forest, bringing with it the crisp smell of snow and ice and frozen earth. The sun was dipping toward the horizon, casting long shadows through the trees. She could see the static of

Karim's wards crackling through them. They must have been out for three hours, maybe four.

Hazily, she remembered Karim's declaration that the magic that had roared through her had something to do with both of them, with the way their magic worked together. Fear sliced through her like a blade across an old wound. It was exactly what she had always been afraid of. That she'd been born of shadow, just as the villagers had always claimed. That she was truly a monster.

She dropped her face in her hands. What was wrong with her? Why did this magic take so much out of her? She was usually so careful not to leave herself vulnerable, not to allow herself to be consumed by her magic, which, until now, had been small, something barely noticeable by others. Something she could easily control. And now twice, power had raged through her like an unstoppable gale. And twice she'd slumped into this man's arms and slept like the dead. She could *not* let that keep happening.

Karim stirred, rubbing a hand across his face as he woke. "What's that look for?" he asked as he pulled himself into a sitting position.

"What look?" she snapped, a little more harshly than she'd intended.

"The one you're giving me now."

"I am *not* giving you a look."

"You look like you want to shove a dagger under my ribs."

She snorted. "If I'd wanted to do that, I'd have tried it while you were sleeping." She tossed a pinecone at him. "You'd never have known."

Karim caught it one handed and grinned. "You so sure about that?"

"I'm supposed to be impressed that you caught that, aren't I?" she drawled.

"Of course." He tossed the pinecone back at her, and she batted it down before it hit her shoulder.

Karim winced as he disentangled himself from the bedroll, then cast a skeptical look around them. "We're not back near the Rendran capital, are we?"

Isabel made a face at him, even though his fear was more than valid. "I don't think so." The pines around them were narrow and more alpine than the forests near the Rendran capital. She thought they were still in the southern mountains. At least, she really hoped they were.

"We might want to pack up and hike along the ridge a way," she said, pointing to where the earth inclined sharply behind them. "That might help me figure out where we are." Again.

He nodded, then pulled himself up, rolled up the bedroll, and strapped it to his pack.

Isabel felt strangely light without her pack. Her jaw worked as she went over the contents in her head, cataloguing the things she'd lost—her bedroll, wrapped bread, cheese, and jerky, her water skin, a change of clothes, a few spare daggers. They had to make it to some semblance of civilization tonight. They didn't have nearly enough supplies to make it for long without a resupply. And she was *not* sharing a bedroll with Karim again.

"Do you think they'll find us again? Your countrymen, I mean," Isabel asked uneasily as they started up the ridge. She didn't like the thought that Gustav's men could open doors across distances, cutting what should have been a multi-day journey into a matter of seconds.

"I don't think so." The usual surety in his voice wasn't there. "At least, I really hope not. The groundwork it takes to track us down can't happen in an instant. It will take them time. Our best bet is to keep moving. To make it to the citadel."

For the first time, Isabel wondered if the wards on the citadel would be enough to keep Gustav out.

An uneasy silence settled over them as they trudged up the slope matted with fallen pine needles.

"So, we're not talking about what happened at the river then?" Karim asked when the silence stretched out. "About what happened with our magic?"

A stone settled in Isabel's chest. "There's not much to talk about," she said shortly.

Karim stopped, an incredulous look on his face. "I very, very much disagree with that assessment, Isabel."

Fear sliced through her. She really didn't want to talk about it. Not when she had no idea what to say. "Why don't we figure out where we are first. Then we can talk about whatever you want once we're somewhere safe."

"Fine." His voice was tight. "I'm holding you to that, just so you know."

She did her best to push down the sick feeling in her stomach. She just wanted to get him to where he needed to go safely, without the Inetians or the Medirans or the chanters or whoever was mixed up in all this getting to him. Then she would be done, and she would never have to think about him or what had happened with their magic ever again.

They moved through the alpine forest, their boots skidding on loose stones and sliding on rain-slick leaves. The sun dipped toward the horizon—total darkness was only a few hours away. Isabel tried not worry. They still had time.

"Wait," Karim said suddenly from behind her. "Look."

She stopped and followed the line of his finger. A puff of white smoke, thick and curling, rose over the trees where the rise dropped into a small valley. A sign of civilization.

"Well, that's the first good thing I've seen all day," she said.

They hurried through the trees toward the rising smoke, their boots slipping on the detritus, then stumbled onto a rutted wagon path. It wound down the mountain and into the valley. Isabel signed in relief. It looked well worn, as if it saw frequent use.

The path evened out as they reached the valley. They moved to the side as a group of men on plodding farm horses passed them. They were dressed in tunics of bright reds, greens, and blues.

"You here for the festival?" one of them called as they passed.

Isabel and Karim exchanged a look. "Of course," Isabel said.

"Village is only a twenty-minute walk that way," another of the men supplied. "You'll be there quickly."

"Thanks!" Isabel called after them.

"Festival?" Karim asked when they'd passed.

"Apparently so," Isabel said. A festival? Where were they? At least the knowledge that there was a village ahead was helpful.

They pressed on, and soon the trees fell away, and the promised village emerged from the mountainside.

Squat wooden houses with thatched roofs lined the road. Chickens wandered in gardens that burst with squash and cabbage and other greens. Lanterns of enchanted orb fire in a variety of colors were strung between the roofs, and children ran through the streets, chasing each other with sticks. Villagers lingered in the lanes, laughing and talking excitedly. The scent of roast meat wafted from somewhere, and Isabel's stomach gave a sudden growl.

Her mind struggled to catch up with what she was seeing. There were more people in the streets than this village could usually hold, she was sure.

"Oh," she said suddenly, clarity washing over her like sunlight. "It's the autumnal equinox. I completely forgot."

Karim glanced up at the sky for a second. "And that's some sort of celebration, I assume?"

She nodded. Not just any celebration. It was one of the most important nights of the year in small communities like this one. A celebration of the harvest and wishing for a bountiful year ahead. Isabel's chest ached suddenly, remembering the whirling dances in her village, the roaring bonfires, the mouth-watering smell of roast hog—how she and her parents and her sister would sit out beneath the stars, looking up at the constellation of Asaragus the Archer as they toasted to a good year ahead.

A two-story building came into view on their right. Isabel stopped, scanning the sign above the door.

"I know where we are," she said, relief crashing over her like a wave. So, she had managed to do something helpful in her rampage of power after all. "This is Medina Acil."

"It's what?" Karim stepped up behind her, peering at the sign above the door.

"Medina Acil," she repeated. "It was supposed to be our last stop before our trek up to the citadel. It's only a few miles from here."

They had once again traveled a few days' journey in not much more than a moment.

Their journey would be over soon. They could bypass Medina Acil entirely and make it to the citadel tonight if they really pushed for it. Karim would be safely ferried away in the mountains, and Isabel could go back to Rendra, back to her old life, back to the only thing she had ever wanted—to move unseen through the darkness, forgotten, her job to fade away into shadow.

"Okay, then," Karim said, a sudden fierceness in his voice. "We're not going anywhere tonight. We're going to sit down, eat some good food, and forget about all this for one night."

Isabel opened her mouth to protest, but he shook his head. "The chanters won't have a read on our location for a few days at least. We're safe for now. And I plan to have some fun for once in my damn life." His eyes bored into her. "And maybe then you'll actually *talk* to me."

Her jaw clenched, and she wanted so badly to come up with a snappy retort, but her mind was blank. They *should* push on to the citadel. The quicker he got there, the better. But they were also tired. And the scent of roast pig was wafting into her nostrils and her stomach was growling. And tonight, she knew there would be dancing—the reels and jigs she had grown up with. The one thing she had been able to enjoy.

Her heart squeezed again, and against her better judgment, she heard herself saying, "Okay."

CHAPTER 7

They were able to get two rooms at the inn, which was a miracle considering the holiday and the wagons that had come in from the surrounding settlements for the celebration. There was a flat area at the back of the village where travelers had pitched tents beneath the trees or thrown canvas tarps over their wagons to create a space for their families to sleep. Small cook fires flickered like fireflies, and some of the travelers were selling small things, from produce to trinkets to jewelry and clothing.

As the sun sank below the horizon, the roasted pig was pulled from the pit where it had been cooking for the better part of two days. Isabel watched in delight as the meat was pulled and prepared, and people gathered around in excitement.

"This reminds me of our celebration of the coming of the rainy season in Ineti," Karim said as they waited in line to get a plate.

"Do you roast a pig?" Isabel grinned.

His mouth tipped up. "Goat, actually. It's hot and dry for most of the year where my clan lives. We get very little rain, so most people raise animals. But when the rain does come, we celebrate with food and drink and dancing."

She tried to imagine Karim dancing and couldn't. She wondered how different the dances he'd grown up with were from the whirling reels and jigs she'd danced in the village. She caught herself watching Karim. She was struck again by how little she knew about him, about his life before all this.

They each got a plate filled with meat, simmered beans, and a plethora of roasted vegetables, as well as a mug of ale. Karim pointed out an empty table on the other side of the bonfire, and they made their way over and sat down.

"All right," he said, peering at her over his mug of ale. His eyes flashed. "We need to talk about your magic."

Isabel rolled her eyes. "I thought you said the point of this little venture of ours was fun."

"I also said my goal was to get you to talk to me."

"You *are* talking to me."

"Isabel."

She leaned back in her chair. "What do you want to know? What happened earlier today . . . I told you already. That's never happened before. Well, except in the Mediran dungeon."

Karim nodded. "I've been thinking about it. About why."

Isabel's shoulders tensed. "And what did you come up with?"

"I told you before that my affinity is weaving wards to make things . . . more like themselves."

She nodded.

"And yours is to draw shadows to you. Existing shadows."

She waited for him to go on.

"It's— I think it's me. My magic. It coaxes yours to be more of itself. More shadow. And it's like"—he waved a hand in the air—"I don't know, we *became* shadow."

Isabel stared at him. Became shadow. A new hollowness settled in the pit of her stomach.

"It's not like anything I've heard of before. Or even read about." His fingers curled around the mug of ale. "It was like our power amplified. Like one fed the other. The more my affinity coaxed yours to become more of itself, the more shadow there was to coax. An infinity of expansion."

A chill spread across her body. "Okay," she said, trying to wrap her mind around his words, trying to keep the panic at bay. "When does this, this magic, transform from the good kind of magic you described before and become something twisted like what the Sorothi chanters practice?"

"I don't think it does," Karim said, taking a sip of his ale. "We aren't forcing things to do what they weren't intended to do."

"Aren't we?" she said. "At some point, the shadow must grow beyond what it was meant to. You said it was an infinity of expansion. So what? We end up engulfing the entire world in shadow? When it dissipates, it must go somewhere." Her fingers clenched nervously and then released. "How long until this blows up in our faces and we pay the consequence?"

He was quiet for a moment, regarding her with a thoughtful expression. When he finally spoke again, his voice was soft. "My grandfather had an affinity for wards and things, like I do. If magic is passed down in a family line, then I certainly got my ability from him. He was the one who taught me to imbue objects with protective wards and the like." He nodded to the knife that still hung at her belt, to the sheath he'd given her that morning. "He coached me to make that. To tell it that it was a dagger, meant to protect. And it seems it's done its job."

The wards in the knife flared briefly at his words, as if it were listening, basking in his approval.

"And what does that have to do with . . . with what happened today?" she asked, a lump forming in her throat.

"I've practiced what the chanters are teaching." He leaned forward, his voice earnest. "I knew from the first moment I saw what they were doing that they were twisting the world to their will, not letting the world be as it was supposed to be."

She watched as more people filled their plates bursting with food.

"You remember the man from today? The one with the scar who tried to convince me to come with them?"

Isabel nodded. He had seemed impossibly sad—a man caught in a position he'd never imagined himself in.

Karim's gaze traveled beyond her shoulder. "His name is Paarsav Amanakar. He's one of Sethos' many cousins on his mother's side, the eldest son of one of the most powerful families in Ineti."

Isabel frowned. She did not envy those who had to deal with the complicated bloodlines of the Inetian throne. "And he was the one who led your group to the Sorothi enclave?" she ventured.

Karim nodded, his gaze darkening. “Paarsav knew my uncle. He knew what had happened to my family—that we’d been sent back to our clan lands in disgrace. He knew my uncle was seeking revenge on the emperor. Paarsav was the one who convinced my uncle and my father to join the cause.” His jaw tightened. “And he was the one who convinced me too.”

Isabel watched him quietly, waiting for him to go on.

“I had my entire life mapped out before me from the time I was born. My father had a prominent position in the Inetian military, and I was to follow in his footsteps as the oldest son. My magic affinity was just something that could help me rise in the ranks even faster. I attended the most prestigious military academy in Ineti, and I *excelled*.” His hand clenched around his mug of ale. “I was poised to rise higher than my father ever had. And then my uncle’s fall from grace came, over nothing more than the emperor’s jealousy. Something so incredibly petty, it’s not worth repeating.”

He continued, an edge to his voice. “I lost my place in the military. My uncle, my father, and our family were sent back to our clan’s lands in the far west of the empire, ostensibly with jobs that were of the ‘utmost importance to the empire’, but that were little more than a means to get our family out of the way.”

He shook his head. "I was angry. Angry that everything I had ever wanted had been taken from me on a mere *whim*. I wanted the emperor to pay. It was not right that someone so full of himself and careless of the well-being of others could sit on the throne of such a vast empire."

"Kind of like the Mediran king," Isabel said.

Karim nodded. "*Exactly*. Except a thousand times worse." He sighed. "What Amanakar was offering seemed like everything I wanted. I could finally use my affinity for something I deemed to be *good*. I thought that anyone deserved the throne more than the emperor himself did. And so Akil and I went willingly, excitedly, to Medira."

He stared out toward the embers of the bonfire. The sun had fully dipped beneath the horizon now, and shadows flickered off his hands and across the table. "We'd only been at the enclave two months before the explosion that took Akil's life." His fingers curled again around his mug. "I knew at that point that what we'd been sent to learn was stupid, dangerous. And I was furious. We'd been used again, and Akil had been discarded, as if his life had never mattered at all."

Sorrow curled in Isabel's gut. What a waste. A waste of life. A waste of skill. A waste of power. A waste of human beings who wanted better lives for themselves, for their families.

"And you know the rest. I'm wanted by seemingly every damn nation that's ever meant something to me." He took a long swig of his ale.

An ache of sadness settled in in Isabel's chest as she looked at him in the flickering light. His entire life had been torn apart by greed and power. He was without a land, without a family. He had made some bad choices, yes, but they had arisen mostly from circumstance. And Isabel could understand that. More than understand that. And yet, he was here with her, life blazing in his eyes, with a desire to stop the injustice that had torn his life apart. Something softened in her chest.

"Do you miss it?" she asked. "Ineti, I mean. Your old life."

He glanced up at her in surprise. "Some things, yes," he said softly. "I miss sleeping with my family on our roof on the hottest nights of the year, feeling the breeze on my skin and knowing that everyone I loved was near." His mouth tipped. "It meant that I was safe, that I could sleep easy. I haven't had a night of peace like that in . . . I don't know how long."

Isabel's mind skittered to his warmth at her back when she'd woken in his bedroll this afternoon, a strange sort of peace and safety settling along her skin. She violently pushed that thought away.

"So, you see," he said. "I know the difference. I can feel it. What happened today and at the Mediran palace, that wasn't magic that was meant to tear the world apart."

Isabel wrapped her arms around herself almost involuntarily. What did it mean if he was right?

He leaned toward her, his eyes blazing with intent. "*Why* are you afraid, Isabel? Your magic is a part of you, of who you are. Isn't that something that's taught in Rendra?"

Afraid. All thoughts of peace and safety scattered to the wind. She hated that he could see through her like this.

"It's not that," she started, trying desperately to keep her voice even, to not let him see how much his words had rattled her. "It's just that *everyone* in my life before I came to the capital was just waiting, Karim, waiting for me to turn into an Archer-forsaken monster. My whole village knew about what I could do with shadow simply because I didn't realize that no one else could do what I could, so I'd never tried to hide it. I spent my childhood being whispered about, pointed at, having other kids called away from me when I tried to join a game."

The old hurt flared in her chest, but the words were coming quickly now, and she couldn't stop them. "My parents told me over and over that I was normal, that the others in town didn't know what they were talking about.

That I was their child and could never disappoint them. But it was hard to keep those other voices out. The ones telling me I was a thing of darkness because of what I could do."

Something wild and angry flashed in Karim's gaze. "Do you truly believe that about yourself, Isabel?"

She dropped her eyes to the plate of food that was growing cold in front of her. She had tried for so long not to believe that about herself. But then her magic had erupted with blackness and power and rage, just as the villagers had always claimed it would, and now she had a hard time pushing those voices away again.

"My sister never believed that about me," she said softly, running a finger absently along the edge of her plate. "Sophia. That was her name."

Karim didn't move.

Isabel's throat closed. It had been a long time since she'd talked about her sister to anyone. "She was two years younger than me. Our parents were good to us—more than good. They loved us unconditionally. I was always the dark, stormy one, but Sophia, she was brightness and laughter. Our mother died when we were young. And then, after our father died, I convinced her to come with me to the capital. There wasn't much for us left at home except to get married and . . . that wasn't an option for me.

Not there. I was sure there would be more work, more of a life for us if we got out, away."

Her voice wobbled. "She was so excited to be in the city, in a place so much bigger than where we had grown up, a place so full of life and people. We had some money and were hired as scullery maids in a larger villa near the palace." Her hands ached at the memory of the endless hours of scrubbing dirty dishes and pots and pans in scalding, soapy water, her fingers raw and cracked, especially in the depths of winter. "It was hard work, but Sophia thought it was all rather exciting. I was willing to put up with it because we needed the income and because she was just so . . . happy."

Isabel picked up her fork and absently stabbed it into a piece of meat. "Then winter came, and she came down with a cough. At first, neither of us thought much of it. Sickness is rampant in the servant's quarters, especially in winter. But it kept getting worse and worse. And eventually she came down with a fever." She could see her sister now, shivering in her bed in the maid's quarters in the heart of the city, her body slick with sweat. "I tried to take care of her between my shifts in the kitchen. I tried to help her, but I—" Her throat closed further, and she shook herself, willing the pain away. She had had almost three years to work through this grief.

"She died," she said after a while. "On a cold day in January. It was snowing."

Karim's gaze was unbearably soft across the table, his features cast in firelight.

"I left my job," Isabel continued. "I couldn't bear to stay there. Too many memories." She shook her head. "I was lost. Alone and grieving. And I knew I couldn't go back to that kind of work, not when I was on my own. So that's when I had the insane idea to . . . get the attention of the queen's shadow. I had nothing left to lose. It was either grasp for the kind of life I wanted or . . ." She trailed off. "Luckily, Cassandra was the type to be impressed with a stunt like that rather than infuriated. She gave me a job, and then rooms in the palace. Everything Sophia and I had ever dreamed of."

"Isabel," Karim whispered. "I'm . . . I'm sorry."

She looked at him then, at the softness in his gaze, the orange light of the bonfire casting shadows along his cheekbones and jaw. Her heart gave a sudden, irrational thump.

"I know you lost your brother," she said quickly. "And I know watching my sister waste away from illness is nothing compared to what you went through—"

"No," Karim said sharply. He learned forward, his gaze earnest, intense. "Don't say that. One loss is not worse than another. You lost your sister and that hurts. Just as much as it hurt to—to lose Akil."

The lump in her throat expanded suddenly. "I've always been a thing of darkness, Karim. Everyone I love . . ." She trailed off.

"You are *not*." Karim's eyes flashed at her across the table, an intensity in them that made her shiver. "You *know* that's not true. You are not a thing of darkness. You are *not* a monster. It's your *choices* that turn you into a monster. And as far as I can tell, you haven't done anything that leads me to believe you are monstrous."

She let out a shaky breath, not daring to raise her eyes to look at him. She had never spoken those words out loud before—her fears, her worry. And now he had come and somehow pried it out of her, and then he had to go and say *that*, as if he could see through her into the deepest part of her soul, to the grief that had lingered there for so long.

She stared at him across the table, and there was something heavy, tangible, hanging between them. A moment she didn't want to break, didn't want to end. Her heart gave that traitorous thump again.

He was the one who finally leaned back. He gave her a shaky smile. "There," he said. "I got you to talk."

Her mouth curved. "Traitor."

His eyes widened for a second, and then he snorted. "You're walking on thin ice there, Algerin."

"Have you ever seen ice before?" she asked pointedly.

"No," he said. "But I've heard it's remarkably changeable."

The heaviness that had hung over her since she'd sprung him from the Mediran prison lifted for a moment. She smiled at him, suddenly feeling strange and giddy and light all at once.

There was a sudden cheer, and a trio of fiddles on the other side of the fire struck up a jaunty tune. People were on their feet in an instant, chattering in excitement as they joined hands in a ring around the bonfire, feet kicking and hands clapping as they fell in step with the reel.

Isabel's heart leaped, and she couldn't stop the smile that spread across her face. She knew this song. Her foot started tapping unconsciously. She hadn't danced in so long. Too long. It had been the one thing she could do at village celebrations where she felt so utterly and totally herself. Where she could move and whirl and forget that she was the girl of shadows, the girl to be feared. In the midst of the dance she could become invisible, part of a whirling whole, where nothing else mattered.

Karim leaned forward, his mouth curving dangerously. "You don't strike me as the type who likes to dance."

Isabel's eyes flashed, and she matched him stare-for-stare. "There's a lot you don't know about me, Saad."

"I'm figuring that out," he said.

There was a beat as they stared at each other across the table, the world seeming to narrow, the space between the infinitesimally small. Isabel's heart gave a thud, and she pushed herself out of her chair.

Karim stared up at her, the orange light of enchanted orb fire casting a shadow along his jaw. Isabel swallowed, then said as lightly as she could, "I remember you saying the point of this night was to have fun. So, I'm going to." Then she turned toward the circle of whirling dancers and thrust herself into the fray.

Her body remembered the steps, the movement of the music, before her brain did. The jigs and reels she had grown up dancing, the energy of the crowd, the laughter, the movement, as the people around her lost themselves in the music. Laughter bubbled up in her throat as she joined hands with one partner and then the next, legs kicking, body whirling, moving in an interconnected circle. For a moment, she could forget herself, forget the darkness of the world, and just be.

Then a hand slid into hers, warm and solid, and Isabel found herself staring up at Karim. He gave her a smile, uncertain and boyish.

"So, you do dance?" she said.

"I don't know if what I'm about to do can be counted as dancing," he said. "But I have danced before."

Isabel grinned. "You'll pick it up."

"Will I?" he asked.

And then the music started again, and they were dancing. It was immediately clear that he didn't know the steps, but Isabel did her best to stay beside him, dragging him where he needed to go, nudging him when he missed a step. He caught on quickly.

And then they were whirling with the laughing, moving crowd, and Karim's face was brighter than she had ever seen it. The reel wound to a sweeping crescendo, and they joined hands and turned away again, clapping to the rhythm, then swinging back again.

They danced another, and another, and then another, until they were laughing and drenched in sweat and gasping for breath, and Isabel couldn't remember when she'd ever felt so light.

Then just as suddenly as it had begun, the music stopped. Cheers and applause echoed up into the night air.

A rush of people moved past them, some heading for their seats while others hurried to join the next reel while the musicians paused for a swig of water or ale. Karim grabbed her arms and pulled her back against the eaves of the nearest house to get them out of the way, and Isabel found herself giggling at the absurdity of it all—the noise and the dancing and the way their magic had flowed together and his hands like fire on her arms.

She looked up at him as the crowd swelled around them, her eyes glowing. He grinned down at her, his cheeks flushed from the dance.

She swallowed, suddenly realizing how close he was, that his face was hardly inches from hers, his hands still gripping her arms, steadying her from the jostle of the people around them. His breath was warm on her face, and she could see the sweat beading on his brow and his pulse beating a rhythm against his throat. There was one beat, and then two, when neither of them moved, neither of them said anything, and the night bloomed around them with life and sound and euphoria.

His gaze darkened, and she was suddenly feverishly aware of everywhere their bodies touched. She knew she should move, knew she should get out of here and run away from whatever it was that was lingering dangerously between them beneath the eaves of a house on an autumn equinox in Medina Acil. Something that she couldn't allow herself to want.

His hands slid up her arms, pulling her closer, and her fingers pressed against his chest, twining into the fabric of his tunic, thundering with the heat and feel of him. Her own pulse roared maddeningly through her body, but she didn't move, didn't pull away, and with a wild kind of terror, she realized that she wasn't going to stop what was about to happen.

"Isabel," he said roughly, his head dipping as his nose brushed against hers. She tipped her chin up, their breaths mingling so close she could almost taste him.

A cheer rent through the night as another reel picked up. They both started, and Isabel leaped back as if she'd been flung from a catapult. What was she doing?

"I— It's late," she stammered. Her eyes were wide, and she was sure her pupils were dilated in the dim light. "We have a long day tomorrow. I should probably—"

He looked like she had punched him in the gut. "Oh. Right," he said. His mouth opened and then closed, as if he were still trying to work out what had just happened. "Long day tomorrow. Rest."

His eyes caught hers for a moment, and that dizzying wave of longing, of desire, came sweeping back over her.

He opened his mouth, his hand coming up as if to reach for her again, but she shook her head.

"Goodnight, Karim," she said firmly, more to convince herself than to convince him.

"Right," he said, his hand dropping back to his side. Isabel could still see the tension coiled through him, the same tension that was winding maddeningly through her. "Goodnight, Isabel."

There was another beat where neither of them moved, and for a moment, Isabel allowed herself to think about what would have happened—what would be happening now—if—

"I'll see you tomorrow," she said shakily.

"I— Yes. Tomorrow," he said.

She turned and fled.

Chapter 8

A cold rain misted through the trees, pattering off the thatched roofs of Medina Acil and streaming down the dirt lanes. Isabel peered into the misty haze, pulling her hood over her head and tightening the straps of her new pack against her shoulders. It was only a few miles to the citadel, but when the often-treacherous mountain paths were slick like they were this morning, they would have to be very, very careful.

Karim emerged from his room a few minutes later, his pack already slung across his back. Isabel gave him a nod as he approached, trying not to think of what had almost happened last night—his breath on her lips, the fire of his body pressed against her own, his sure hands holding her arms, pulling her close against him.

He gave her a stiff smile. "Sleep well?" The bags under his eyes told her that his night had been just as restless as hers.

"I slept great," she said. "You?"

"Like a rock."

They set off into the rain, Karim a few paces behind Isabel. The entire village was still asleep after last night's carousing, which had lasted late if the music and laughter from outside her window had been any indication.

She'd tossed and turned all night, unable to get him out of her head. And when she'd finally fallen asleep, her dreams had been littered with the Inetians on the riverbank, with the soft curve of Karim's lips as he'd smiled at her in the light of the bonfire, with the surge of the shadow power raging through her. She wasn't sure which had been the most terrifying.

Today she would take him to the citadel, just as she'd promised Cassandra and the queen. She would do her duty. Last night had just been a been a moment of headiness brought on by the energy of the crowd, by the things he'd said to her that had made her feel seen for the first time in her life, by his closeness and the way he'd smelled. By the way she'd imagined her fingers in his hair, his lips against hers, his— She ground her teeth in frustration. She was doing it *again*.

The path narrowed and climbed steeply as they moved away from Medina Acil, trekking deeper into the mountains. Isabel's legs were burning by midmorning when the misting rain finally cleared, and the sun peeked its way through the clouds. A soft warmth settled over her, and it wasn't long before any previously chilled parts of her body had warmed in the sunshine.

It was Karim who finally motioned for them to stop. She had been pushing them hard. They were so close. And she didn't want to stop to let herself think about anything else. Anything to do with him or with her magic or with the fact that she really, really didn't want to be alone anymore.

Karim dropped down onto a nearby log and pulled out his water skin. Sunlight filtered through the branches of the pines, casting bronze rays along his wavy black hair. He took a long swig before capping it and putting it back in his pack. Isabel lingered a few feet away, her pack still on her back.

"How far are we from the citadel?" he asked, breaking the silence that had been prickling between them all morning.

Isabel peered along the sloping path, which disappeared around a rocky outcropping at the edge of the trees. "Another mile maybe, not more."

He nodded. His eyes bored maddeningly into her back, but she did her best not to look at him.

"Are you going to sit down?" he asked, his voice tight.

"I'm fine." Her stomach gave a traitorous growl.

"Just sit down and eat something," he said, frustration tinging his tone.

She grudgingly did as he told her, sinking down onto a pockmarked stone boulder not far from where he was sitting. She removed her pack and dug through it to find the bread and cheese she'd squirreled away from Median Acil. She was hungry and tired. It had been a long few days.

Karim took a bite of cheese from his pack. "So, when we get to the citadel, what happens?"

Isabel forced herself to meet his eyes. "Once I open the way for you, you're in. You'll be able to stay there, safe behind the wards." She paused. "Cassandra will send regular couriers with updates and questions pertinent to our situation."

Karim looked at her. "Will you be one of those couriers?"

"I might," she said noncommittally. It was a possibility that Cassandra would send her back, especially if something truly disastrous occurred. Her job had been to keep an eye on the Inetians in the dungeon. She'd done that. And with the men gone, it would likely fall to her to continue tracking them down—and that probably entailed further interaction with Karim. But now, she needed to get back to the palace to inform Cassandra about what had happened at the river—and that Gustav would keep coming for Karim.

At least in the citadel, he would be tucked away where they would never find him.

She wrapped her arms around herself, staring up at the mountain. Suddenly, she understood Karim's reluctance to reach the end of their venture. It would mean another end to his hard-won freedom. This time, he wouldn't be in a squalid prison like in Medira, but he still wouldn't be free. Her heart ached for him. Life hadn't gone the way he'd thought it would, but he still hadn't lost that spark, that resilience, that conviction of what was right.

"I wish—" she started, emotion rising in her like a wave. "I wish . . . " She didn't know what she'd meant to say. There was nothing she could say. Nothing that wasn't some fanciful, idealistic future where kingdoms and politics and consequences didn't matter.

"You wish what?"

She shook her head. "It's nothing. Just stupid." She stood abruptly and pulled her pack onto her back. "The citadel is just ahead," she said before he could say anything, then turned and marched into the trees.

Isabel was thankful that the rain had stopped. The rocky trail was already slick, and her boots slipped more than once as they climbed.

The path ended abruptly in a sheer cliff of jagged gray stone. A few ragged trees clung along its face, but, for the most part, it was sheer. Unscalable. They stared up at it, at the wards crackling through it. These wards were very old and very powerful. They had protected kings and queens in ages past in times of warfare and strife. And now they would protect Karim too.

"How is anyone without magic supposed to get through this?" Karim asked from behind her.

"You just have to know where to look."

Isabel moved to the left side of the path and pressed her hand into a jagged ridge in the stone, then whispered the words Cassandra had taught her. For a moment, nothing happened. Then the wards in the stone flickered, and a narrow, spiral staircase materialized in the rock. Isabel blinked. She could still see the cliff face in front of her, but there was clearly a staircase as well, as if both things existed at the same time.

Karim whistled. "That's an incredible piece of magic. Whoever did this managed to convince both the cliff and the staircase that they exist. The precision required for something like that is . . . mind-blowing."

"The old mages of Rendra and Medira were very, very powerful," Isabel said quietly. For the first time, she could understand why Gustav might want to achieve this kind of magic—these wards were beauty and precision and balance all woven in one. It was breathtaking.

Isabel gingerly set her foot on the first step of the staircase. It was a strange feeling to watch her boot slide through the stone. But the stair beneath her boot was solid, so she pushed herself fully into the rock face.

They emerged into a sunlit courtyard that brimmed with trees and green and life. A great white oak sat in the center of the cobbled path, its trunk so wide that Isabel didn't think she and Karim together could reach all the way around it. The garden was ringed on one side by a white stone tower, and on the other by an elegant colonnade. Between the elaborately carved pillars, Isabel could see the southern mountains in all their glory.

Isabel swallowed. She hadn't had time to really wonder at the beauty around them when they were trying to find their way up. But now, she was struck by the brilliance of her own kingdom. Of the miles, the distance they had traveled over the past few days. Of the beauty of the delicate wilderness around them.

A short, balding man limped out of one of the doors that led into the colonnade. His dark hair was speckled with gray, and he was dressed in a faded brown tunic and leggings. He gave them a curious look as he made his way down the colonnade and out into the courtyard.

"Carlos Luca?" Isabel asked. She pulled the sign of the queen's shadow from beneath her tunic and held it where the old man could see it. "I am Isabel Algerin. I have come to deliver this man into your care at the behest of Elena, Queen of Rendra."

"Ah, good," the man said. "Then you've come to the right place."

***

Luca led them along the colonnade and into the citadel tower. He hadn't asked why Karim was here or what it was that he needed protection from. He'd simply smiled and said that knowing the queen required his protection was enough.

They followed Luca through a curved hallway lined with paintings of the kings and queens of Rendra, heavy wooden doors interspersed at intervals. He showed them the kitchen, which was stocked with all manner of meats, cheeses, breads, canned goods, and dried fruits. He kept a garden in the courtyard, he told them, that was currently brimming with squash, broccoli, and winter greens.

Isabel lingered at the door when Luca brought Karim to his room. It was unexpectedly large, with a plush red-and-gold tasseled rug that disappeared beneath an ornate four-poster bed. A velvet chair perched under a square window that looked out on the mountains.

Karim dropped his pack in the room as Luca rattled off a list of information—water could be drawn from the well in the courtyard and heated for baths; firewood was piled beside the hearth but there was more in a vestibule down the hall. Karim would be required to help with tasks around the citadel—chopping wood, cooking, and tending to the gardens.

"Is there a library?" Karim asked, his eyes sparking with interest.

Luca nodded. "An extensive one. Though I don't think you'll find anything out of the ordinary in it. But you're welcome to browse."

Isabel was glad to see, at least, that the old man was kind. That Karim wouldn't be alone. And that the citadel would be a better kind of prison than the one he'd been stuck in in Medira. At least, that's what she kept telling herself.

She glanced out the window. The sun was lower than she wanted to admit, and a sheen of rain clouds had moved in again. She knew she should go. Had to go, in fact, if she wanted to be back in Medina Acil by dark. But she lingered, telling herself that it had started raining again, and she didn't want to march right back out into that. That she needed to make sure she'd seen her job through to the end.

Luca offered her food for the return journey, which she gratefully accepted, wrapping dried meats and cheeses and placing them in the pack she'd acquired in Medina Acil.

Karim followed her back to the courtyard, to the spiral staircase they had entered from. Neither of them said anything as she spent too much time securing her water skin to her pack, too much time fiddling with the straps, making sure it was snug against her back. Too much time not thinking about what had to happen next.

"So, I guess this is it then," she said when she had run out of things to check.

Karim stood rigidly a few paces in front of her, his hands slack at his sides. "I guess so."

"I'm sure I'll be back," she said in a rush. "We still have a lot of unanswered questions. And Gustav is still out there. They'll probably try to come for you again."

"They definitely will." For a moment, that boyish look was back, the one she'd seen in the Mediran dungeon—a little boy afraid of the dark.

He ran a hand through his hair, as if he were deciding what to say. Finally, he sighed. "So, you really don't want to understand what our magics can do together?"

Isabel swallowed. This again. The one thing that scared her above all else—except maybe for the emotions he'd awoken in her, emotions she thought she'd battened down when Sophia died. "You've seen what can happen when magic goes awry," she said, hating how small her voice sounded. "I'd rather not end up like Gustav, always searching for the next hit of magic, of power."

"You know it wouldn't be like that."

"Wouldn't it?"

He stared at her for a moment, a hardness in his gaze. "You still don't trust me, do you?"

She opened her mouth to protest, but then shut it again, suddenly unsure of her answer. She wanted to trust him. She wanted to trust him so badly. But the truth was, she couldn't even trust herself.

"Do you trust anyone, Isabel?"

"Yes, of course," she said, but her mind was scattering in all directions. Trust. How could she possibly trust when everyone she had ever loved had disappeared or rejected her? If she threw herself into his arms now, it would still all just end. And she would be left with nothing again.

"Who?"

She wrapped her arms around herself, wanting to curl into a ball and disappear from the face of the earth.

"Who, Isabel?" he pressed when the silence stretched on.

"Cassandra," she bit out, but the name sounded weak to her own ears.

"Do you really?" he asked, his voice hard. "Because when we left the palace, you told me not to reveal my magic affinity because those in power would use it against me. Is that the reason you haven't told them?"

"Fine," she ground out. "I find it very difficult to trust anyone."

He crossed his arms. "Especially me, it seems."

Anger surged through her then, at herself, at him, at the things the world had thrown at them both. "I have no one, Karim!" she burst out. "No family. No friends. No one who cares for a single moment if I'm sucked through a rift for all eternity! In fact, there are a lot of people back home who would claim I deserved it, for being the shadow girl, that I'd brought it on myself."

He shook his head, tension simmering in every sinew of his body, but when he spoke, his voice was soft, which was so, so much worse than if he had snapped at her. "Things happen in life, Isabel. Bad things. But we must be better than them. We can't let them turn us into angry, bitter shells of what we could be."

An angry, bitter shell. That's *not* what she was. She was trying the best with what she'd been given. And she thought she'd been doing a damn good job.

This couldn't be the way it ended between them, all prickly silence and avoidant gazes. But it had always been like this for Isabel. Everything good had always ended. And now this would too.

"Here," she said, pulling his knife from her belt. The wards twined up her arm with a tender warmth, like an old friend. "You should have this."

Karim stared at the knife in her hand. He shook his head. "No." His eyes flashed with a sudden intensity.

"It's yours. You made it." Her fingers tightened on the hilt as she held it out.

"I did make it. But it's yours now. You need it far more than I do."

The lump in her throat rose again. "Are you sure about that?"

He reached out and closed his fingers around hers. He pushed the knife back toward her. "I'm sure."

Their gazes locked, and Isabel thought she might cry. It was unlikely she would ever feel his hand wrapped around hers like this again. And that was not a thought she'd allowed herself to entertain until it was staring her right in the face.

A moment passed in which neither of them moved. Isabel knew that as soon as she did, she would have to turn away, she would have to leave, and he would stay here, and all this, everything between them, would be over.

She was the one to move first, the one to break his gaze, to step back and shove the knife back into its sheath on her belt, just as she always was. The disappointment in his gaze was palpable. She had to leave soon, or she was going to do something really, really stupid.

"Goodbye, Karim," she said, an echo of her goodnight the evening before, when the whole world had seemed to open to her for one brilliant moment. "I'm sure I'll see you again."

"Yes." His smile was sad. "I really, really hope so."

Isabel turned away, and slipped into the staircase, her hair already damp from the misting rain. It wasn't until she had exited the citadel and made her way into the dense canopy of trees that she allowed the tears to fall.

She had only been walking for ten minutes when the wards in the knife gave off a loud warning pulse, the shock waves of power vibrating through her body as the forest was bathed in a wash of wrongness. Bile rose, hot and sour, in her throat. A strange white light, like the one she had seen in the dungeon in Medira, radiated from the citadel behind her into the misting rain. She turned and saw that the wards had turned an ugly mottled red, great faults opening through them like a spiderweb made of fire.

Isabel gave a strangled cry and threw herself back up the hill, back toward whatever terrible magic was smashing against the ancient wards of the citadel, and back toward him.

It was the only right thing she had wanted for years. And now she had another chance.

Chapter 9

Isabel flew up the mountain path, her legs burning, her breath coming in heaving gasps. She had to get back to the citadel, back to Karim, before it was too late.

Another flare of white lit up the sky, casting strange shadows beneath the trees. Almost without thinking, she called them to her so that they pooled around her ankles and twined up her legs, scattering the brightness in her wake.

She had once been so sure of the old wards, sure that they would hold, but after what she had seen in the Mediran dungeon and by that riverbed, she wasn't so sure anymore.

A strange laugh escaped her lips. She had been so afraid of herself, of her magic, for so long. But it had never been something she'd needed to fear. It was a part of her that came as easily as breathing. A part of her she could no longer ignore.

A deafening crack rent the air, like ice breaking apart in the winter, and all at once, the mountain flickered, the cragged peaks melting away to reveal the white stone tower of the citadel. Isabel's stomach turned, fear washing over her in a single, striking wave. The wards had protected the Rendran citadel for hundreds of years had been broken.

She ground to a halt at the base of the cliff. The perfect balance that had been struck by the old mages all those years ago had been tipped, and the staircase that had been so well hidden spiraled up the stone in full view. Veins of red scattered up the face of the citadel, spreading like molten metal through cracks in porcelain.

Fear whirled through her. She should have seen this coming. She'd known Gustav would stop at nothing to get what he wanted. And he wanted power. Karim's power. She shouldn't have been so eager to leave, to flee, to get as far away from Karim and the flurry of emotions he'd stirred in her.

She shouldn't have been so afraid. And now, she might never be able to show him that she wasn't a coward.

With a cry of rage, she threw herself up the staircase, taking the worn steps two at a time, praying she wasn't too late.

She burst out into the courtyard, her chest heaving as she scanned the citadel for any sign of life. A cry tore from her chest when she saw a body lying twisted on the ground. Carlos Luca. She rushed forward and crouched down by the old man. She didn't bother to check for a pulse. His neck was twisted at an odd angle, and his eyes were wide open, his mouth locked in a silent scream. Isabel's stomach heaved, and she scrambled back away from him.

Where was Karim? Panic flooded through her, and she tried not to imagine him twisted on the ground like Luca. Tried not to visualize his black eyes staring lifelessly up at her.

A strange boom echoed off the mountain, and the red cracks in the wards pulsed again. The door Luca had shown them through when they'd first arrived was hanging at a strange angle from its hinges, as if it had been kicked or blown off.

Isabel sprinted through the colonnade, then made her way down the curved hallway beneath the watching eyes of the old kings and queens. Shadows rushed up around her, and she shivered at the smooth, cool feel of them against her skin. She hadn't realized how many she'd drawn as she'd run. They followed her like the train of a fantastical gown of darkness, and she didn't have time to think about what that might mean.

There was another flash of light, another wave of the acrid scent, followed by the muffled shouts of men's voices. She flew past the door to Karim's room and clattered up a curved staircase. She yanked Karim's knife from her belt, the wards twining up her hands. The shadows around her legs jumped at the influx of power.

She burst into the lavish reception hall Luca had shown them through before. A wide balcony overlooked the courtyard below, where she knew Luca's body still lay. Her heart gave a sudden thump when she saw Karim standing in front of the stone railing, his hands raised, power crackling along his arms and through the dagger in his right hand. His hair was wild, standing on end from the buildup of power that twisted through the citadel.

A dozen men were scattered around the hall, some with short swords drawn, others with hands raised in the same manner as Karim. Isabel recognized Paarsav's broad form at the head of the group. Ankar, with his angular face, was beside him.

"This is really your choice, Saad?" Paarsav was saying, his sword raised in front of him.

"My *choice*?" Karim shook his head in disbelief. "You're not giving me any choice, Paarsav."

Paarsav's shoulders tightened, but he didn't back down.

"You all know that man is a monster!" Karim's voice carried urgently across the space. "He's using you, using your power to get what he wants."

"Shut your mouth!" Ankar snarled.

Karim glared at him. "We are better than this. We are Inetians, born of the land of the sun. We come from clans with power, lineages that stretch back generations. We don't need *him* to prove ourselves."

"And what do you propose we do if we defy him, Saad?" Paarsav said, his voice tight. "Last I checked, we were wanted in just about every corner of the world."

"We make a new place for ourselves!" Karim said vehemently. "Without him. Without his power. We are all better men than this!"

Paarsav hesitated for a moment, an awful mix of desperation and hope and fear flickering in his gaze. Like Karim, he had just wanted a better life—and he'd been trapped by Gustav's lies.

"I know you didn't want any of this," Karim pressed. "I need your help, just as you need mine. Don't go through with this."

Paarsav stood like a man frozen, his dagger clenched tightly in his fist. Isabel could sense the tension in him. The indecision. The longing for something more than the lot he'd been thrown in life.

The angular man spat on the floor. "Listen to yourself, Saad. Talking as if you're better than us. As if you wouldn't decide to save yourself when it came down to it."

"I am not better than you," Karim said. "We all made choices to ally ourselves with him. We all decided the risk was worth it on our own. And I've paid for my stupidity many times over. We all have. What I'm saying is that we don't have to keep making that same decision repeatedly. We have an opportunity to stop this madness, to forge a new path for ourselves."

"Coward," Ankar hissed. And with a sudden howl, he threw himself at Karim.

Isabel was running before she had time to realize what she was doing, but the space was vast, and Ankar collided with Karim, knocking him to the ground. She gave a cry of rage and yanked the shadows that huddled in the farthest corners of the hall to herself.

"Don't move!" Paarsav barked to the other Inetians.

A few of them hesitated, exchanging glances as Karim slashed at Ankar with his dagger. Ankar spun away, then swept Karim's feet out from under him. Karim went down with a startled yelp, the knife skittering from his hand and over the edge of the balcony.

Fury and terror flared in Isabel's chest, and she flooded the hall with darkness, shadow billowing in waves. Yells of confusion echoed through the hall, and Isabel was moving, flying under the cover of darkness to the place she knew he was. She didn't have any plan, anything beyond the knowledge that she had to get to him, that she had to get him out.

Then she was beside him. "Karim," she breathed. She gripped his forearm, so she knew where he was in the darkness. She could just make out the angular lines of his face only a few inches from hers.

"Isabel?" he said incredulously. "You came back."

"Why do I always have to save you?" she said roughly, gripping his hand and hauling him to his feet.

His mouth quirked in a way that made her pulse quicken. "Maybe it's because I'm your damsel in distress."

Isabel snorted. "Well, I'm going to get you out of here, princess. Even if it means I have to tear this entire place to pieces."

"That's the nicest thing anyone has ever said to me."

She grinned back at him, then let her hand slide down into his, ready to lead him back through the darkness and out toward freedom, away from the citadel with its broken wards, from the Inetians and Ankar, who wanted nothing but death and ruin. For a moment, hope flooded her veins, and she thought they just might have a chance of escape.

A sudden chill swept through the hall, and Isabel's shadows dropped, skittering back into the corners she'd drawn them from. She whirled, trying to call them back to her, but they were already scattering. Fear stabbed through her gut. What was happening?

A white-haired man with snow-pale skin stood at the top of the staircase at the end of the hall. He was dressed in a heavy gray robe, and a leather belt with a nasty-looking curved sword hung from his waist. His straight hair was pulled sharply into a tail at the nape of his neck. Ice-blue eyes peered out of a face that was all sharp angles, and Isabel suddenly realized that he was probably younger than the whiteness of his hair implied—maybe only fifteen years older than her. A haze of strangeness seemed to drip off him, as if he'd been stretched thin, and there was something now missing that should have been there.

Isabel didn't even have to question who this was—Gustav.

The Inetians had picked themselves up after the dissipation of Isabel's shadow. Ankar grinned in elation. Paarsav stood not far from where Isabel had last seen him, tension radiating from every sinew of his body.

"I don't understand." Gustav looked slowly around the room. His voice was gravelly, as if something had torn through it long ago. "I expended all that energy to take the wards down, and I find that Saad hasn't even been apprehended yet."

The Inetians jumped. Even Paarsav straightened, his eyes trained on the chanter.

Isabel's blood boiled. What a pompous, narcissistic ass.

"I'm glad to finally see you again, Karim," Gustav said, his smile cold.

Karim tensed. "It's always a pleasure, Gustav."

Isabel reached for her shadows a second time—she could feel them now, still distant, but less out of reach. Her brows knitted together. What kind of magic did this man possess that he was able to keep her shadows from answering her call?

Gustav's eyes flicked to Isabel, as if he could sense what she was trying to do. A chill moved down her spine. "Who is this?"

"She showed up with Saad a few days ago in the forest, sir," Ankar said, taking an eager step forward. "Seems to have some sort of magic affinity."

Gustav's eyes pierced through her. "Where *did* you find this one, Karim?"

"I thought it was me you wanted," Karim hissed, taking a slight step in front of Isabel.

"Oh, I do." Gustav's mouth twisted. "You don't have to worry about that."

"Then leave her out of this!" Karim's fists clenched. "Leave them all out of this."

"No." Isabel stepped forward, laying a hand on Karim's arm. He looked at her in surprise. "I'm not letting you get all noble on me. I told you I would get you out of here, and that's exactly what I came back to do."

She turned to Gustav, fury burning through her. "You think you have the right to control the lives of these men, but you do not. They are free to make their own decisions. They don't need you to do it for them."

Gustav's brows rose. "Are they?" He turned then to Paarsav. "Get them already, will you?"

Paarsav hesitated for the second time that day. Gustav's eyes snapped to him, coldness building in his gaze. "Paarsav. I asked you to get them for me."

There was a new wildness in Paarsav's gaze. "No," he said, and drew his sword.

Isabel lunged for Karim just as Gustav's face twisted in rage. Her fingers wrapped around Karim's, his hand warm and solid in her own, and she could already feel the crackle of power rolling through him, jumping from his fingers into her own. Immediately, her shadows rose. Elation rolled through her like a wave, and she sent a wall of darkness toward Gustav, the power raging through her like a storm.

Gustav was knocked back, and Paarsav rolled away, unharmed.

All chaos broke loose as the Inetians drew their weapons. A few scrambled to help Paarsav to his feet, and power crackled through the room again as some of the Inetians began to chant.

Isabel gasped as power built in her again, crackling between her and Karim at an alarming level. The old fear cut through the elation again, the fear that she would lose control and destroy everything around them. The fear that she was a monster after all.

As if he could read her mind, Karim's fingers tightened on hers. "You are not a monster, Isabel," he said, his voice low and urgent in her ear. His warmth beside her was strong and sure, and his eyes were alight with fury and rage and purpose. "But you are incredibly powerful. And that's nothing to be ashamed of."

That's nothing to be ashamed of.

"Let's get this bastard," she said, her eyes blazing into his. She would not be afraid anymore. His mouth curved.

Power flared through her again in a sudden, streaming cascade, and for the first time, she truly allowed it to build. Her nostrils flared, and a strange, electric laugh bubbled up in her chest. She had never felt so *free*.

The air shimmered with darkness and crackled with streaks of power as the energy raged through them, thundering across the stone and wind and space, filling the air with a rushing, whirling darkness.

Gustav gave a guttural cry, throwing his hands in the air, words spewing from his mouth like ashes from a sputtering fire. Isabel planted her feet as the wave of power rolled over them in a suffocating storm.

She could hear other voices now too, joining in the fray, feel a bolster of power as the Inetians rallied around them, lending power and strength to their own. Her heart gave a wild beat of elation, and for the first time she allowed herself to hope.

She sent another wall of shadow barreling toward Gustav, who stood with his arms raised, his mouth moving, his shoulders tensing from the strain.

The Inetians were shouting now, their voices muffled, but she thought she heard Paarsav roar to help them, to do whatever they could to stop Gustav. Karim grunted beside her, but he was grinning when she glanced over at him, his eyes wide and blazing and full of life.

Gustav was powerful, but he couldn't stand against them all.

He seemed to realize that at the same time as Isabel, and he shifted his stance. His words changed suddenly, and the power shifted to something darker and older and far more terrible.

Isabel drew more power, pulling it from Karim, pulling the shadows in the citadel and the earth and the forest around them.

The shimmering white line of a door opened in front of Gustav. He cast a measured look back at the space Isabel occupied, her hands raised, an army of shadows gathered around her, ready to crash over him like a thunderous wave, ready to destroy him.

He stared at her for a moment, a moment in which Isabel hesitated.

You are not a monster, Isabel. It's your choices that make you monstrous.

Gustav smirked, and his eyes flashed in a way that said, "I knew you were too weak." And then, he stepped through the door, taking the crackling power with him.

"Take me with you!" Ankar screamed, throwing himself at the space where Gustav had been, where the door still shimmered strangely against the whiteness of the stone.

Isabel opened her mouth to shout, to tell him to stop, to turn back. But before she could, the door collapsed, snapping the edges of the world together in a clash of light and power and sound.

Ankar's severed body dropped, blood pooling in a garish stain of red, stark against the white of the stone.

The Inetians around the hall stilled, and someone swore.

Power surged again through Isabel, raging and roaring and desperately searching for release. Her limbs vibrated with it, searing with energy until she thought she would burn up. Fear stabbed through her.

"Isabel?" Karim's voice sounded far away, as if he were shouting at her from a distance.

His arms wrapped around her, and she could hear his voice saying something, words that had no meaning, not here, not now, amid this power and shadow and darkness. She was a thing of flame and night, burning up from within. She had to release this power somehow without burning through whatever and whoever was around her. It was the kind of power that would annihilate all it touched—power that had been meant for Gustav. She had to find an outlet, and it couldn't be the citadel or any of the Inetians or Karim. Especially not Karim.

An idea built in the back of her mind, something so insane, so impossible, she could hardly let herself hope. She would not become what people had always told her she was. She was more than their words, more than her fear. The shadow did not control her.

You are powerful. And that's nothing to be ashamed of.

She slipped her arms around Karim's waist, allowing herself to bury her face in his chest, to lean into the comforting feel of him. She didn't want to forget this, forget any of it.

His arms tightened around her. "Isabel," he rasped. "You don't have to carry this alone."

"I have to do this, Karim," she said. Her voice sounded far away, as if she were underwater.

"You don't!" His voice broke as his arms tightened around her.

"If I don't let go, the power will flow out through you. I don't know what it will do."

"I can take it. We can take it together!"

"I can't risk killing you, Karim! I can't!"

Shadows curled up and around her fingers as the vortex churned and spun. She clenched her teeth against the intensity of it.

All at once, she gave a cry and pulled away from Karim. The shadows roared, flaring up into the sky, and with a manic laugh, she stepped into them, so she was moving, floating through the hall and out so that she hung above the courtyard, above the citadel, with the vast splendor of the mountains spread around her.

Now here amid her shadows, she could see it, the place where Gustav's door had been. The space still shimmered, the earth still groaning as it tried to repair itself. There were still cracks, slivers in the fabric, where shadow might slip through.

It would work. She could send the shadow after him, through the door, where it might find him and engulf him or else dissipate into nothing, but it would be out, away, and no one she loved would get hurt.

With another shout, she thrust her hands downward. The shadow roared, and then the whole vortex was moving, bearing down on the space where the door had been. Isabel gave a sudden, crazed laugh as the shadow slid through. It was working!

The vortex raged as the power burned, and she thought she wouldn't be able to hold it, that it would flare out and destroy everything around her.

Suddenly, voices sounded from below, power curling into the air, crackling around her in a veil of safety, surety, and strength, and a memory of Karim's words whispered through her mind: *You don't have to carry this alone.*

She gave a sudden, giddy laugh. *She wasn't alone.*

And then the vortex of shadow was roaring away, the last of it dwindling out of her, slipping through the cracks in the fabric of the world, until she no longer felt like she would tear apart at the seams. As the shadow drifted away, she dropped closer to the tile until her feet touched the ground. Then, like a light snuffed out, it was gone.

She slumped to the floor, alone in the center of the hall.

She was still here. The power hadn't burned her up. She was alive.

Hysterical laughter burbled up from her belly, and she lay on her back on the cool stone of the citadel, basking in the sheer insanity of it all.

"Isabel!" A voice sounded from somewhere, but she couldn't move, couldn't think, as the exhaustion rolled over her.

"Isabel!" The voice came again, this time closer, and then Karim was there, his hands were sliding along her arms, his fingers touching her cheek, her hair, his dark eyes so close, so real, so raw and worried.

"Karim," she whispered.

There, in the warm embrace of the hall, Isabel leaned into his arms, at once whole and good and right.

"You're alive," he whispered against her hair. "You did it. You didn't let the shadows consume you. And you're alive."

"I am," she said hazily. Gustav was gone—whether dead or weakened or just gone, she didn't know. But for now, they were *safe*.

And then her vision was swimming, and she clung to Karim, to his warmth and solidity, and then everything went dark.

CHAPTER 10

Isabel woke feeling like she'd been run over by a horse. She groaned as she shifted beneath the blankets, her body one giant ache. Blankets. She was in a bed. Her eyes snapped open.

"You're finally awake," a familiar voice spoke beside her.

Isabel sat up and winced at the sharp pounding in her skull. Karim was sitting on a plush velvet chair next to the bed she was nestled in, still dressed in the leather tunic and black boots he'd been given in Rendra. He looked like he'd washed and shaved, the black stubble that had shadowed his jaw the last few days suddenly gone.

It took her a moment to recognize the room as the one that Karim had been assigned when they'd first arrived at the citadel. The ornate four-poster bed stretched above her, and she could see the brilliance of the mountains through the window behind his chair. The sky was blue—no longer the hazy gray it had been when she'd slumped into sleep.

"How long was I out?" she asked.

One of Karim's arms was thrown nonchalantly over the chair back. "Two days."

"Two days?" She gaped at him.

"Yes. I knew you'd come to eventually. You always have." He said it lightly, but Isabel could detect the worry in his voice.

The memory of the power that had raged through her returned in a rush—the way her body had burned, as if she would break apart. Then her shadows as they'd poured through the spaces left by Gustav's door, and the way she'd stumbled forward and collapsed into Karim's arms. Again.

"Why does this never happen to you?" she asked. "Aren't you expending magic when we work together too?"

"I don't know." He shrugged. "You seem to be a conduit somehow. My magic just amplifies everything."

Amplifies. That was an understatement.

"So, I'm the one who has to pay for it?" she grumbled.

He grinned. "I don't know. I'd give anything for a two-day nap."

She raised her pillow as if to toss it at him. Suddenly, the realization that she was sitting in a bed, staring at him, caught up to her, and her cheeks flamed. He must have been the one to bring her here and keep watch over her for two long days and nights. There were bags under his eyes, and she wondered how much sleep he'd gotten. A confusing mix of emotions surged in her at the thought.

She could hear men moving around outside the door, and she realized that the Inetians must still be here too. They'd turned on Gustav. It had only been because of them that she and Karim had stood a chance.

Her stomach growled. "I should probably eat something," she said.

"I can bring something in here for you," Karim said. "This place has a lot of provisions. Unsurprising for a royal fortress."

"It's all right," Isabel said hurriedly. "I can get up and find something. I'm not a complete invalid."

"Are you sure? What you need is rest," he said pointedly.

"I just slept for two days, Karim."

"You did."

"And believe me, walking around will be better for me than just sitting here."

"Will it?"

She shot him another look. "Otherwise, I might have to burn energy by shoving your own dagger somewhere you probably wouldn't like."

He snorted. "Fine, then." He motioned for the door. "Let's go."

She hesitated a moment, glancing down at her tunic and leggings—the same ones she'd been wearing two days ago. "Let me just wash up a little first."

"Oh, right," he said, jumping to his feet. "There's a washbasin in the corner. And if you check the drawers in the chest there might be some fresh clothes. They might be a little big, but it's better than nothing. I'll go to the kitchen and see what I can find." He made his way to the door.

"Karim," she said. He paused and turned to look at her, his wavy hair falling across his eyes. He reached up and pushed it to the side. Her heart gave a sudden thump. "Thank you," she said.

His gaze softened. "I really am glad you're awake." He turned and left the room, closing the door behind him.

Isabel sat back, savoring the warmth and stillness. Another confusing mix of emotions washed over her when she noticed Karim's wards wrapping securely around the room.

She had to get out of bed and face whatever was waiting for her out there—the Inetians and their fall out with Gustav, Karim and his idealistic words that had made them stay. They couldn't stay in Rendra. They were wanted. And Rendra couldn't risk its alliances by harboring them. But that didn't mean Isabel couldn't help them, that she couldn't turn a blind eye to what they were doing now.

She dragged herself out of bed, her bare feet sinking into the ornate rug on the cold stone floor. She splashed her face with water from the basin in the corner and did her best to clean herself. She opened the top drawer of the chest skeptically and pulled out a faded blue tunic and white leggings that wouldn't be so bad with a belt cinched around her waist. They would have to do until she could get back down to Medina Acil.

She emerged from the room a little while later, feeling a little less gross. Her stomach gave another enormous growl as she padded along the hallway, trying to remember where the kitchen was.

She pushed open a wide, ornately carved wooden door on the other side of the courtyard and stepped inside. A few of the Inetians were gathered around a long table by the window, and Isabel was struck again by how young most of them were. Heads turned as she entered.

"She wakes!" one of the men cried, raising a tankard of ale in her direction.

The rest of the men gave a hearty cheer, and Isabel gaped at them, heat flooding her cheeks. Karim appeared from around the corner, his eyes twinkling.

The Inetians pulled out a chair and waved for her to have a seat. She slid into the open chair, and Karim pushed a bowl of warm stew across to her while another of the men handed her a spoon. Isabel hardly waited a moment before she was eating, shoveling the food in more quickly than she'd intended. The banquet in Medina Acil felt like it had happened weeks ago, not just days.

"How did it feel to wield shadow like that?" one of the men asked, leaning forward curiously. "I've never seen Gustav so pale!" A few of the men laughed.

"You're our hero, you know." Another man grinned.

"A hero?" Isabel arched a brow. "I don't know about that."

"You made that asshole turn his back and flee," the man said. "Best thing I've ever seen."

"Come on, you lot. Give her some space," Karim said as he slid into the open seat beside her. "She's had a rough few days."

"We've all had a rough few days," the man who had toasted her when she first arrived said, taking another swig of his ale.

"More like a rough few months," another man grunted. The men sobered.

Isabel's chest squeezed. These men had had lives, families, homes, they'd left behind in Ineti. The likelihood of them ever returning was very low. And now they would have to go to another new place, on the run once again. Forever.

"Well, we're free of that bastard now," the first man said. "I'll take that any day."

As she ate her stew, she learned that after Gustav had escaped and she'd collapsed, the men had worked to clean up the mess left behind—namely the bodies of Luca and Ankar. They'd decided to stay in the citadel to gather their bearings and decide what to do next. The wards may have been destroyed, but the stone walls of the citadel and the rocky crags of the mountains remained as a safeguard.

Paarsav stepped into the kitchen and stood near the door. His face was drawn and tired, as if he carried the weight of the world on his shoulders. The group quieted immediately, and a band of tension tightened over the space.

"I'm glad to see you're finally awake," Paarsav said, nodding at Isabel. "And it's good to finally meet under less . . . tense circumstances." He glanced at Karim. "Karim tells me you've been an immense help to him."

Isabel's cheeks warmed. "I suppose so," she said.

"I'd say rescuing me twice counts as helpful," Karim said. His knee touched hers briefly beneath the table and stayed there. She didn't move hers away.

"Karim, I need a word," Paarsav said.

Karim nodded and stood up, then followed Paarsav out into the hall.

"What was that all about?" she asked the men.

The man who had toasted her when she'd first walked in pressed his lips together. "The two of them have been at odds since Gustav disappeared. Paarsav wanted us to be out of here the moment things settled down. Karim insisted we waited until you woke up. We were all exhausted anyway. It didn't make sense to drive ourselves into the ground." He nodded at her. "And now that you have woken up . . . well, we'll see."

We. Of course, Karim was going with the Inetians. It only made sense. He was on the run, just as they were. He had the protection of the Rendran crown, but Rendra couldn't hide him forever. If he were ever discovered, the queen would have no choice but to give him up. And Karim knew that as well as Isabel did.

Isabel stirred her spoon through the half-eaten stew. It suddenly didn't look as appetizing as it had before.

The men continued to cajole each other, laughing and talking with more enthusiasm than she'd expected from people who had just been through the kind of dark abyss they had. But this was also the most freedom they'd had in months, and compared to the Mediran prison, she was sure it felt like paradise.

She finished her bowl of stew and excused herself, leaving the men to their ale.

Karim was walking back down the hall when she left the kitchen, glowering with frustration. He smiled when he saw her, and his face cleared slightly.

"What did Paarsav want?" Isabel asked as he reached her.

Karim sighed, glancing around them. A few of the men were leaving the kitchen now, heading toward the courtyard. "I— Let's go somewhere else before we get into any of this."

She fell into step beside him as they made their way through the circular hallway, then up the curving stone steps and into the grand hall at the top of the citadel. The walls curved elegantly to match the half-circle shape of the tower, and the floor was tiled with white and blue marble.

Isabel shuddered. The last time she'd been there, it had been teeming with darkness and rage and power. A strange dissonance still hung in the air in the place Gustav had disappeared.

Karim led her through the hall to the balcony that overlooked the courtyard, their steps echoing as they walked. The mountains spread out below them in breathtaking splendor, and out in the distance, Isabel could see the snowcapped peaks of the Malathi pass on the border of Rendra and Medira. The sun still lingered high above the horizon, and a brilliant sapphire sky spread out above them.

Karim leaned back against a stone pillar, a soft breeze rustling his hair. He tipped his head back and closed his eyes for a moment. He looked immeasurably tired. He let out a soft breath, and her heart gave a sudden thump as their eyes met. She was suddenly terrified of what he was going to say.

"Sorry," he said, smile pulling at his lips. "I didn't want to be overheard. Things haven't been particularly pleasant around here."

"I've noticed," she said.

"Paarsav and I do not agree on several things. He has no qualms continuing to use the type of magic we learned in the Sorothi enclave, despite its dangers."

Isabel looked at him in the light of the midday sun, at the lines of tiredness that played around his lips and eyes. She understood his frustration, his reluctance after what had happened in the Sorothi enclave. But she could also understand Paarsav's stance. The Inetians couldn't stay in Rendra. They had to leave, to get somewhere as far away as possible to start a new life for themselves. And opening a door, using the power of the Sorothi chanters, was the best way to do that quickly, without leaving a trace.

"They aren't Gustav, Karim," she said softly.

Karim let out a breath. "I know," he said. "I know. I just—I can't do it. Knowing what can happen." Pain flashed across his face, and Isabel knew he was thinking of his brother. It hadn't been all that long since the accident had happened. The pain was still raw—a fresh wound. And Isabel knew from experience that time didn't always make the pain go away.

"It's okay," she said. "I wouldn't want to either, in your position."

He met her gaze then, and there was a softness in his eyes that made her want to reach out and touch him. She wrapped her arms around herself, letting her eyes wander back out to the mountains. "So, you think we're safe from Gustav, then?"

He nodded. "Gustav's not likely to come after any of us. At least, not any time soon. He's powerful, but not powerful enough to take on all of us alone. He's better off starting over, finding other ways to procure the information he wants."

Isabel didn't want to think about him popping up again any time soon. But she also didn't doubt that he would—she just hoped that wherever he landed, someone would be equipped to stop him again.

"Paarsav's plan is to open a door somewhere far away, deep into Elanar or even into Zhonghua," Karim said. "Somewhere Ineti won't bother to come looking. He wants to start a new life there." He paused, a shadow darkening his face. "We all know we can never go home."

There was nothing she could say to that—nothing she could do to make any of it better for him.

He gave her a sad smile. "I came to terms with that a while ago."

"But it doesn't make it any easier."

He shook his head. "No, it doesn't."

They were quiet for a moment, staring out into the shining mountains. Isabel's heart squeezed again. She knew what had to happen next. No matter his differences with Paarsav, he would go with them. They were his one remaining link to home.

And she . . . she would go back to Rendra, back to Cassandra and the queen and her life in the palace.

For a moment, she thought about what it might be like to go with Karim, to step out into the great big world with someone else at her side. What it would feel like to always be able to laugh with him, to curl up with him on cold nights, to have his arms around her, to run her fingers through his hair and— She swallowed and pushed those thoughts away as quickly as they'd come. She didn't get those kinds of endings.

"You—you're going to go with them," she said before she lost her nerve. "You're their best hope for survival out here, Karim."

"Am I?" he said.

"You understand what they've been through," she rushed on. "You have more power than any of them do. They need you."

His jaw worked as she spoke. Her heart thundered painfully in her chest.

"I just—" she started, then stopped, searching desperately for the right words. "I just don't want you to be alone again, Karim. They're your people. From your homeland. And you can't return there. You belong with them."

"And what about you?" he said stiffly.

"What *about* me?" She avoided his gaze.

"You're going to go back to Rendra, to that palace, and forget about all this? About your power? You're just going to live life exactly as you did before you—" He broke off and ran a hand distractedly through his hair.

"I don't know," she said. The ball of pain in her chest tightened.

"Tell me that that's really what you want, Isabel," he said.

Her mind settled on her small room in the palace at Rendra with its warm comforter, narrow desk, and tall window that looked out over the practice yard. Her nights nestled there alone as she mapped out her next job for the queen, trying hard not to think about her sister, about her magic. And the many nights on the road, sleeping with one eye open, always watching her back.

It had been a life. Far better than the existence she'd been eking out before Cassandra.

But now, Karim was standing in front of her, so close, his eyes vibrant and filled with desire and want and hope, and she couldn't bring herself to say anything. Because she did want another kind of life. She wanted him.

Karim let out a breath. "I'm not going to let you do this again, Isabel," he said, his voice low, raw, rasping with emotion. "I have no one. We both have no one. And the one person I do want to have is you."

Her head snapped up, and her body flared with heat. Had she heard him correctly?

His eyes were wide, wild almost, and she could sense the frustration radiating off him. "Not them. Not anyone else. You."

Isabel swallowed; her heart pounded a painful rhythm against her ribcage. "But how would that even work, Karim?" She hated the way her voice sounded—so small and desperate and scared. "I work for the Rendran queen's shadow. I've sworn to protect the crown."

"So, we do it together," he said vehemently. "I already have the queen's protection. We find a way to make Rendra safe. We find out what our magic can truly do. We find a way to use it to better the world, not to harm it."

She wanted so badly to believe in that reality. She wanted so badly to believe that it could exist.

"What about Paarsav and the others?" she asked.

"They're strong." Karim's gaze was unwavering. "They don't need me."

Her mind reeled, fear and want warring in her chest. "What if someone comes for you?" she whispered.

"Then we run."

There was so much surety in his voice, so much confidence in his stance, so incredibly certain that everything would work out, that everything would be okay. The way she had never been able to believe it would be.

"Isabel," he said. "It's not about the things that might happen. It's about making a choice. And I've made so many bad ones in my life. But they've brought me here. To you. You're my one good choice."

Her blood rushed wildly through her veins. A choice. She had always had a choice—like she'd had when she'd faced off against Gustav in the hall of the citadel. She'd always been able to choose to be more than what the village women had claimed she was. She wasn't a thing of darkness and shadow. She was Isabel. And she could choose to have the kind of life she wanted.

She didn't have to be afraid.

Her heart expanded suddenly with hope and light, chasing away the shadows that had huddled there for so long. Her fingers shook as she closed the final distance between them, not allowing herself to think anymore.

His eyes widened, and then his arms were around her, and he was whispering her name, his body like fire against her own. Her fingers dug into the soft fabric of his tunic, and then his mouth was on hers, soft and gentle and full of want, and she was once again shadow and flame brightness, all at once exactly what she had always been meant to be. Her arms slid around his neck, grasping at his hair and his tunic and his back, pulling him closer, as if she were dying of thirst. His hands slid down her body, and a shiver split through her at his touch.

Time passed in a slow cascade, and when he pulled back, Isabel could hardly remember where they were. His eyes were glazed, and a lazy, satisfied grin wandered across his mouth. Isabel wanted nothing more than to drag him back against her and never stop kissing him.

"Was that a decision?" he murmured, his breath soft against her cheek. His thumb trailed gently along her collar bone, and she felt it like a shock wave down to her toes.

"I don't know," she breathed, her fingers tracing the soft skin at the back of his neck. "We might need to try that again, so I can be sure."

"Right." His forehead dipped to rest against hers, and she could feel his smile against her lips. "Just to be sure."

Another while later, she was the one to pull away.

"We'll make our way back to the Rendran palace, then?" she said. His hands slid along the curve of her waist, and he kissed the soft space below her ear. She suddenly forgot what she'd been about to say.

He pulled back, a wicked grin on his face. "We will," he said. "Eventually."

"Eventually," she echoed, leaning into him. "No need to hurry."

"None at all," he murmured, and then he was kissing her again on the balcony of the Rendran citadel, the broken wards of the old mages crackling around them, and despite the host of unknowns that lay ahead, Isabel had never felt more wholly sure that tomorrow would dawn brighter than it had before.

***

A few hours later, Isabel stood at the top of the citadel with Karim as the sun dipped below the horizon, their hands twined tightly together. Below, in the courtyard, Paarsav and the remaining nine Inetians began to chant, their voices joining with the flickering remains of the old wards. A thin line of light split the air above the place where Carlos Luca had died, spreading outward as the door opened, shimmering faintly in the fading light. One by one, the men stepped through the door, disappearing to a location only Paarsav knew, somewhere far from the citadel, and far, far from the land they had once called home.

Finally, Paarsav was the only one remaining. He looked up to where Karim and Isabel stood on the balcony and gave them a final nod. Karim's shoulders tensed as the Inetian turned and stepped through the door—the last real connection he had to home, to the life he'd once known.

A few moments later, the door flickered closed—softly, quietly—leaving no trace of the Inetians behind.

Beside her, Karim let out a breath, then reached over and pulled her back against him. She leaned into him, allowing his warmth to wrap around her as he buried his face in her neck.

They had a long road before them still—one of discovery, of finding where they fit in the world, of learning of their magic and how they could use it to change the world for good.

Isabel wrapped her fingers around Karim's where they rested at her waist. For once she was no longer alone. And the world was no longer as shadowed as it had once been. Because they would face it together.

And that was enough.

Epilogue

One Year Later

Isabel beamed down at the simple band of silver on her finger, still not used to the way it felt against her skin. Karim had bought it for her from a stall at the autumn equinox festival in the last town they'd passed through, sliding it on her finger with a grin that had made her flush down to her toes. Then they'd flitted hand-in-hand through the stalls beneath the strings of colorful orb fire until they'd found the village elder, who'd been surprised but delighted to perform a hand-fasting ceremony on such short notice.

That night they'd dined on roasted mutton—a specialty in the western Alliance lands—and a plethora of other hearty dishes. They'd written Sophia's and Akil's names on a scrap of paper before tossing them soberly into the bonfire in remembrance. Then they'd retired early, though they didn't sleep until much later that night.

Isabel had never imagined she'd get married so far from her tiny village in the north of Rendra. Never imagined that she'd get married at all. But then, she'd also never imagined most of the things that had happened to her in the past year either.

After the Inetians had left through Paarsav's door, Isabel and Karim had made their way back down to Medina Acil, and then finally back to the Rendran capital—without a boost from her shadows.

Cassandra and Arphaxad had been troubled by the news of Gustav's disappearance but didn't ask too many questions about what had happened to the rest of the Inetians. The Mediran king was still in an uproar about the escape, but Lady Salandris had done an impressive job of talking the king down, even when the Inetian emperor had expressed his extreme disapproval.

"I think she's even better than you were at this, dear," Cassandra had said to her husband, giving him a playful pat on the cheek.

"Well, thank goodness I was ordered to marry you," he returned, his eyes sparkling.

"Thank goodness, indeed," Cassandra had said.

The Inetian emperor had been predictably livid about the entire situation, and relations between Medira and Ineti had cooled considerably. Which had been a headache and a half for Rendra, though it seemed the Inetian emperor was starting to think that maybe Rendra was more worth his attention than Medira was.

The queen had been disappointed but understanding when Isabel had turned in her notice. Isabel knew she owed a lot to Cassandra and the queen for giving her a chance to prove her worth, but she also knew that Karim had been right—there was a lot to figure out about their magic. And no one nation—even one with a good-hearted ruler such as the Rendran queen—should have access to the kind of destruction Isabel had wrought in the hall of the citadel.

Ever since the confrontation with Gustav—and probably before that even—her shadows had been different, more reactive, more palpable. Even when she wasn't touching Karim—and she'd been touching him a lot more lately—they rose up with hardly more than a thought. Something had shifted since her shadows had first started rising, and she wasn't fully sure what it was.

She and Karim had wandered together through Rendra and into the Alliance lands, searching out forgotten texts and listening to gap-toothed elders speak of magic that was used to help and to heal, old stories that had been passed down through generations. They'd spent nights sifting through Isabel's shadows and striving to understand more about how Karim's wards worked. They wove wards of peace and calm and protection into items villagers brought to them in exchange for food and a place to sleep.

A few times, Karim spoke of looking for Paarsav and the rest of the Inetians, and Isabel always kept her ears open for word of a strange band of warriors looking for a home.

But most of all, they had been happy.

There were times when the old fear of her shadows returned, and there were times when Karim was wracked with nightmares of his brother, of a horrific rift torn in the fabric of the world and the dark things that came through it. But every time, they were there to hold each other and tell each other it was going to be okay.

Now, in a small village in the far west of the Alliance lands, Isabel twisted the silver band on her finger, the shadows of the deepening night wrapping around her like a warm embrace. Karim stoked the flames of their cookfire, then came to sit down beside her.

"Hey," he said, pulling her against him, his lips nestling in her hair.

"Hey," she said. She leaned into him, allowing his familiar scent to wash over her.

Warmth moved through her in a wave, and it had nothing to do with the heat of the fire. This was where she belonged—her whole life had been spent drifting between shadows. But now he was here with her, drifting through the shadows together, so she didn't have to wander alone anymore.

She leaned up and gave him a quick kiss at the corner of his jaw. His arms tightened around her. "I love you," he whispered.

Isabel couldn't help the smile that spread across her face. She stopped him as he leaned down to kiss her. "I love you too," she said.

Then she pulled his face back down to hers and kissed him beneath the flickering shadows in the clear, moonlit night.

READ THE NEXT BOOK IN THE SERIES

THE EDGE OF BRIGHTNESS: THE CHANTERS NOVELLAS 3

She's a princess with a broken engagement. His proposal is too tempting to refuse.

Sahar Raddan is the daughter of the Inetian emperor. When her arranged engagement is broken, she's no longer considered marriage material—or good for much at all.

Then Jianyu Liang, an obnoxiously handsome noble from distant Zhonghua, arrives in her city and makes a shocking proposal: a fake engagement. He'll use his status to return Sahar to favor if she helps him track down a missing book of ancient magic—a book he believes was stolen by the great traitor of Ineti . . . who also happens to be Sahar's brother.

With nothing left to lose, Sahar agrees to Jianyu's proposal and is swept into an intricate game of intrigue, lies, and dangerous magic. Now Sahar and Jianyu must work together to recover the book before it falls into the wrong hands, while also contending with their growing feelings for each other—and whether their engagement is quite so fake after all.

Available on Amazon.com or rachelsongauthor.com

Sign up for my newsletter at rachelsongauthor.com

ACKNOWLEDGEMENTS

Thank you to my wonderful husband Michael Song, for his unending support and for pushing me to be better at everything I do. You're my alpha reader and my copy editor. Thank you for putting up with me as I talk through plot holes and go on tangents about characters.

I would not be the writer I am today without the amazing ladies of my critique group, Abigail Ford and Michelle Dobson. You guys are full of knowledge, wit, and hilarity, and aren't afraid to give me honest and much-needed feedback, as well as pep talks to get me out of a writing slump! Our frenzied, endless evenings of writing sprints have pushed me to get more words out with more consistency than I ever imagined possible. You've laughed and cried and fangirled over my writing, and I could not have done this without you.

I also want to extend a thank you to my mentor in all things editing, writing, and publishing related, Pamela Gossiaux. You believed in me when I had no direction, showing me that I could make a career out of my passion for writing. You've been endlessly helpful with your knowledge of the publishing industry and what it takes to get a book out there!

And finally, thank you to my parents, Steven and Monika Lamine, for encouraging me in all my endeavors, allowing me to read and write and travel the world to my heart's content.

About the Author

Rachel Song is a fantasy romance author and fiction editor, and has been an avid writer and reader since she was eight years old. She remembers gleefully huddling under the covers with a forbidden flashlight, reading until the wee hours of the morning. Some of her favorite authors include Jane Austen, Juliet Marillier, VE Schwab, Sherwood Smith, Megan Whalen Turner, Garth Nix, and J .R.R Tolkien.

Rachel lives with her husband and son in metro-Detroit, where, when not writing, she can be found reading, cooking, gardening, traveling, and playing something adventurous on her PS5.

She is the author of *The Chanters Novellas* series, and you can learn more about her and her books at rachelsongauthor.com.

Made in the USA
Columbia, SC
25 July 2024

38827351R00105